Who's Gonna Love You?

Blue Storm Publishing
2417 Welsh Road
Suite, 21 #119
Philadelphia, Pennsylvania 19114

Printed in the United States of America.

This book is a work of fiction. Names, characters, places and incidents either are products of the author's imagination or are used fictitiously. Any resemblance to actual events or locales or persons, living or dead, is entirely coincidental.

First published as a paperback with Blue Storm Publishing 2015

Library of Congress Cataloging -in-Publication Data

Lindsay, Kim M.

Who's gonna love you / Kim M. Lindsay

I. Romance, African American- I. Title.

ISBN 978-0-9965670-0-8

Acknowledgment

God always puts a song in my heart, dreams in my head and missions that seem so impossible! With His unfailing love, protection and soft spoken guidance, I would never have been brave enough to try and accomplish the many things He told me I could.

I thank Him eternally for trusting me with who He made me to be, the gifts He imparted in me and the ear to hear Him reassure me of His love.

Who's Gonna Love You?

A Novel by

KIM M. LINDSAY

Blue Storm Publishing

• Philadelphia •

"You're never limited in what you aspire to do.

You just have to try harder and perhaps take a different path."

~Kim M. Lindsay

For:

Bernice who said one day that:

Rod was her Sun,

Kim was her Moon

And

Nor was her sea of Stars.

That makes her our Universe!

Mom

·PROLOGUE·

Fourteen year old girls in yellow and blue sweaters with the letter R sewn on the front of them cheered with matching pleated miniskirts.

R-O-O-S-E-V-E-L-T!
Let's hear it Roosevelt Junior High!
Let's Y-E-L-L it to the sky!

Scotch Plains is taking you down, down, down town!
Maxson Junior High!
Plainfield is going down, down, down town!

The girls chanted and twisted their bodies cheering for their eight grade football team hoping they would beat the better team, Maxson Junior High.

Maxson was from the next small town over, Plainfield. No matter how loudly they screamed, cheered and kicked their legs, they were crushed and Maxson took home the win.

Andrea Moore was one of the cute girls in the pleated skirts rooting for Roosevelt to no avail. After the game was over Andrea was walked home by her sweetheart Jonathan. They lived on the same street and often walked home together.

With pom-poms swinging underneath clutched books in front of her, she walked slowly to make it last.

He was a cute boy from a good home with loving parents. They lived in an upscale town where fathers were professionals and mothers had a nanny if they chose to work.

In the 80's the quaint town in New Jersey still experienced unlocked front doors, no drugs and a rolled up sidewalk at dusk.

Jonathan was average size for a fourteen year old boy who walked, talked and acted all of his fourteen years. He loved Andrea from the first day he saw her in the third grade. He was her first kiss and he thought they would be together forever!

They walked past their neighborhood park where they were seen by a group of kids from school who rushed over to make fun of the love birds. Andrea didn't care because she knew all of her girlfriends at school envied her because she was Jonathan's girl.

The gang of six or so kids stood in front of them making kissing noises and whistling. One of them, Greg Butler, just stood watching the couple and didn't join in the teasing. When the gang didn't get a reaction from Andrea or Jonathon they started to move on until Greg stepped forward and asked Jonathan a question.

"Why you goin' with her man?"

Jonathan looked at Greg trying to figure out what the question was about. Then he tried to walk past Greg not answering the question. Andrea followed Jonathan. Greg walked behind them and continued,

"I wanna know why she's with you? She fly and you gay looking."

Greg then walked in front of them to cut them off. Jonathan just squinted his eyes at him while shaking his head to dismiss Greg.

"What you gonna do if I say I like her? What if I say I want her to be my girlfriend?"

Jonathan couldn't believe what Greg was saying because they barely knew him and Andrea was in fact his girlfriend. The crowd of kids watched in disbelief at Greg's revelation about liking Andrea. Andrea just stood and watched not knowing what to say or do.

Greg stepped past Jonathan to address Andrea. "You like me?" he questioned.

In that moment she was scared of Greg, so she didn't answer him; she just looked up at him. He was tall and a lot bigger than her Jonathan. Greg wasn't cute at all to Andrea. He didn't play sports and wasn't achieving in school. He didn't live on their side of town and didn't hang out with the popular kids.

Now Greg stepped back in front of Jonathan. "Well, she like me 'cause she didn't say no. So looks like she gonna be my girlfriend from now on. What you wanna do 'cause if I have to fight you first then let's go," Greg said confidently.

Andrea's heart was beating fast. She couldn't believe these boys were going to fight over her right there on the sidewalk.

"I don't wanna fight you Greg, that's stupid," Jonathan finally said.

"Wow, you a punk! You ain't gonna fight for your girl? That's why you shouldn't have her. Here's your last chance to prove you ain't no punk in front of your girl. Let's go!"

Andrea was hoping at this point that her boyfriend would drop his book bag and punch Greg in the face, but he didn't. Instead, he turned around and walked away. The gang watching all roared with laughter and yelled about what had just happened. They all watched Jonathan's back as he walked away.

Greg strolled back up to Andrea who was still standing there holding her books and pom-poms. She was wondering what was going to happen next.

"I like you and I just proved how much. Your boyfriend might have kicked my ass out here but I took that chance. I thought he would have been mad enough to try, but he didn't. I would have respected him if he tried, and then I would have left you alone. Well, he's gone now, you my girl or what?"

Andrea gave Greg a shy half smile while looking him deep in his eyes. And she was his.

· 1 ·

ANDREA

"*Dad*, I want to come home!" Silence on the other end of the dorm's pay phone. "Dad, did you hear me?"

She leaned against the hallway wall with the pay phone between her ear and shoulder while looking at her fingernails and picking at the acrylic coating that was starting to rise from her natural nails. She dropped the calling card she was balancing between her fingers to be able to pick at her nails. The card landed face up showing her printed name, Andrea Moore, along with the digits to dial to make a call from any pay phone. The issue date next to her name was August 1988, just before she entered Boston University.

"Yes, Andy, I heard you, but you need to try and stick this out. College is hard for all freshmen. You just need to make friends and

1

build your life and get the job done. You remember what the job is, right?"

"Yes, Daddy, my job is to get good grades and then the prize, an education. I know all of that. I just want to come home for a few days. It's so lonely here. It's hard, and I…"

"I know sweetheart, but if I rescue you from school you will continue to depend on us to fix things, and that just isn't the real world. I've made that mistake of just giving and giving to you and letting you off the hook. Now, you can't cope when you're out of your element. When things don't go exactly the way you want them to, you don't work it through. Lorraine and I are getting on with our lives now that you are on your way. You know the big plans we have of cruising and remodeling the house; well, we want to start those plans. We've always lived very well, but we wanted to do so much more. We wanted to get you raised and through school, so we could live out our dreams."

Andrea knew the words her father was speaking were straight from her stepmother's mouth.

"Now, Andy, we've done our part, so you have to do yours. You have plenty of money on the Visa, and you'll be able to bring your car next year. We're here for you, but you have to grow up. Give Lorraine and me a chance to miss you. Lorraine has been like a mother to you and has taken good care of us. I don't know where we would have been if she hadn't come into our lives all those years ago after your mother passed. Give her some time alone with me. You know we love you." There was a long pause.

"I tell you what, give it a month and we'll revisit this conversation. How about that?" her father suggested.

She didn't really know what she wanted, but Boston University wasn't it. She needed more time to figure it out and wanted to do the figuring in her own house with all the familiar things that made her comfortable. One of which was her new car that she was given for graduation. She was missing her friends and the life she had at home. College wasn't what she thought it would be. No one knew her and didn't care to know who she was or where she came from, she thought.

Her dad broke another pause with, "You have a few days 'til the weekend. I'll call you back on Saturday and check on you. Okay?"

"Okay, Daddy," she sighed. "Goodbye."

"Goodbye, pumpkin."

Slowly Andrea walked back to her room from the hallway. Her father had given her money to have a private phone installed, but she decided she wouldn't bother since she didn't plan to be there much longer.

Her wheels were turning as she made her way back to her room. She needed a solid plan that would get her back to Scotch Plains, New Jersey and back to the comforts of having a housekeeper, lots of friends, and the time to lay poolside whenever she wanted just by stepping out of her backdoor during the summer.

Boston University was a larger world than she expected. She always knew that she was supposed to go to college. But after the first week, Andrea made up her mind that some college would be enough. She decided that she would settle down with a man who could provide for her as well as or better than her father had after only finishing a year or two of college. But now, after several weeks, she was realizing that she couldn't make it that long. She wanted to go home now!

She plopped down on her queen-sized bed in her private room that was a condition she had for her attendance at Boston U. Her father was an alumnus, and he did everything to get her in despite her mediocre grades. He bribed her with the private room, the bed, and the car she received as a graduation present from high school. Rolling over on her back, she pulled one of her pom-poms from a shelf above

4

the bed and began to stretch a few of the plastic strings until they snapped. This was soothing while she thought hard about a plan to get her out of Boston.

Pictures of her, her friends, keg parties, and football games plastered the walls of her dorm room. Andrea had been on a cheerleading squad of some sort since she was a little girl. Some girls were into dance, but cheering was her thing. The last time she was on the field wearing her red and white lettered sweater and pleated miniskirt was when she was her high school's captain of the varsity football cheering squad. In all of the photos on the walls, she looked like she was having the time of her life, and she was. In a large picture above her bed that hung over the shelf where her pom-poms sat, she was on top of a standing pyramid with the squad. Because she was petite, she was always on top of the stunts, and she loved the attention.

Andrea was five foot three with mocha brown hair streaked with natural light brown highlights. Her hair was well below her shoulders straightened but seemed a little shorter in its natural state of small spiral curls. She preferred to wear it blown straight with a hot handheld dryer and whipped into a high ponytail. She hated the fact that any humidity would revert her straighten hair back to spongy curls. Her perfectly smooth skin was caramel colored that had a glow of pure perfection that came from youth and good genes. She had a heart-shaped face, baby doll lips, and beautiful long eyelashes which she inherited from her mother. She was indeed a looker, and she knew it.

When Andrea was in high school, she and her girlfriends had a very active nightlife despite their squeaky-clean daytime image. Girls with access to money and free run of the world found it easy to do just about anything, anywhere. Weekends were spent dressed up in designer clothes and expensive jewelry with Victoria's Secret underneath. They sprayed their neck with the best perfumes, the exact copies of their mothers' collections. From the time the first of them received a driver's license, they were mobile and able to take the party beyond Scotch Plains. They were able to travel from New York City to any New Jersey shore line party town to Virginia Beach. They flipped from football pep rallies with bonfires to hanging out on the weekends like fully grown women. They were fearless and took risks their parents knew nothing about. A few would take up with older men who didn't realize they were barely 18 years old. Because they presented themselves as expensive packages, some men assumed they were older. Andrea's closet of designer dresses, shoes, and jewelry would make most grown women envious.

In her upscale, affluent suburban town, kids gathered friends of every ethnicity. The prerequisite for being a part of the popular group was not to be black like her, just popular. She left behind a boyfriend she had dated throughout high school off and on. He wasn't a Scotch Plains boy because she thought the boys from her school were too close to home and would be in her every day. She dated the quarterback from their football rival in a neighboring town, Plainfield High School. He was the most popular guy at his school, and his good looks didn't hurt. Their parents were friends and had many friends in common, so it was a desirable match. They came from the same world and understood everything about how they were supposed to act and be. Both sets of parents thought their pairing was acceptable and encouraged it. No one knew or noticed that they didn't love each other, they were just convenient for each other. Appearance was more important to both of them than genuine love. Andrea would have stuck with him if they were not the same age and if he had been established and able to take care of her. But, he was off to Rutgers

University near home in New Jersey, and it would be years before he was making any real money, she knew.

After the traditional graduation bash down the shore, Andrea and her quarterback agreed that would be the last time they'd claim to be a couple and the last time they'd have sex.

Loud knocking came strong through the metal dorm door.

"Who is it?"

"Me, you dirty girl, open up," a female voice rang through.

Andrea thought to herself, *I'm no dirty girl. What does that mean, anyway? She sees my private room just like hers, and it's clean. My parents have money too!*

Andrea got up slowly, making LaTrice wait as punishment for calling her a name. Once inside, LaTrice started complaining that all Andrea did was lay around.

"Get tup, gal. Geez, all yah be doin' is layin' round, child," she said in her best Jamaican accent. LaTrice was Jamaican born and raised but only put her accent on when she was being funny or was around other Jamaicans. She was a tall skinny 22-year-old student with long box braids. She was the first person Andrea met on campus and the only one she had formed a relationship with, since she spent all her free

8

time pouting in her room. LaTrice seemed to have all the trappings of being supported by parents with means similar to Andrea's parents.

"What? What do you want, LaTrice? I've only known you a few weeks, and you're already getting on my nerves!"

"How is that? You look like you lost your dog or something. Let's go out and have fun. There are so many guys here in Boston," LaTrice shot back.

"Where? I haven't met any yet. They all look like college dorks."

"Not the guys here on campus. There are some fine brothers at the local clubs! I get numbers every weekend, and they always want to wine and dine me so they can get back to my room."

"Well, I'm not down for that!" Andrea snapped.

"No, stupid, you don't have to do what you don't want to. Just get your wine and dine on, that's all. Have some fun. If you don't want to see them again, well they can't get into the dorms unless you let them in. I figure I'll get what I want outta the deal, if I give my time. That's just smart business!"

"That sounds like trickin' to me, LaTrice."

"No, it's not. It's being smart, so you're not giving it away. Be it your good stuff or your time. It cost to be with me either way," LaTrice said while snapping her finger in the air. "Plus, my dude is back home on the island, and he only visits every three months or so. I need more attention than that. He'll be here soon, and then I'll have him wine and dine me."

Andrea thought that the way LaTrice was bragging about her love life was strange. It didn't add up for her that LaTrice's boyfriend was so committed that he came to see her all the way from Jamaica and took care of her, but she still saw other men. It didn't seem like LaTrice was in love; maybe she was just hanging onto her boyfriend while she looked for a bigger fish.

LaTrice rattled on and on about how great her boyfriend was. Andrea rejoined the conversation and joked with LaTrice, but she really thought that LaTrice was not on her level. Based on the things LaTrice was saying, Andrea knew she had no class. But, since LaTrice was the only friend she'd made so far, she figured she would tolerate her for now.

Saturday came, but there was no call from her dad like he promised. Andrea broke down and called home. Her stepmother answered the phone.

"Oh, hi, Lorraine, it's me. I was expecting a call from Daddy."

"Oh, dear, how are you?" Before she could give an answer, Lorraine kept talking. "He's out playing golf today at the Scotch Hills, that country club he loves. The weather is nice here, so you know he was headed there this morning."

"Well, did he tell you that I wanted to come home for a few days?"

"Yes, he mentioned it to me, but it sounds like you are doing fine."

"Huh? What makes you say that? I only said where's Daddy and that I want to come home!"

"Well, sweetheart, Daddy did explain our situation, right?"

"What situation?"

"That we are entering the second half of our lives, and we have a lot we want to accomplish now that we are no longer taking care of you."

"Lorraine, I want to come home, like tomorrow. I need a few days to just think about whether this is the right place for me. So I'm not asking. I'm coming home."

"Andrea, look, we've done our very best for you. I think we gave you too much and made it too comfortable for you. It's time you stand on your own two feet. I think you just want to get back here so you can create an adult life living at home with all the ease that comes with living here free."

Andrea took a stronger tone, "Lorraine, I'm coming home tomorrow!

"I'm sorry, Andrea, but tomorrow doesn't work for us. Let's talk about it in a few weeks. A lot can happen in that space of time. You'll make some friends, and I'm sure you'll decide that you love it there. Before you know it, you will have built your own life. I mean we are not asking you to work and contribute to your expenses and tuition. My parents didn't pay a dime for my college. I had to work and make my own way and, frankly, I was thrilled to be out on my own."

Andrea was getting angrier by the second as her stepmother's speech went on and on. While Lorraine was lecturing her, her thoughts went somewhere else. Andrea saw Lorraine for who she was from the beginning. She may have worked hard and paid her own way in college, but, less than a year after Andrea's mother died, she had roped her father in so she'd never have to work again. Lorraine had been her father's secretary and knew him well even before her mother's illness. Lorraine was a very attractive white woman with a slim figure, long bouncy blonde hair, and electric blue eyes. Her mother becoming ill and dying was a lucky coincidence for Lorraine. Andrea believed Lorraine was after her father since the day he hired her and probably would have ultimately taken him away from her mother anyway. Cancer just sped up the inevitable outcome.

Andrea's patience with the conversation had worn thin. Lorraine was still talking when Andrea came back from her thoughts about Lorraine's intentions towards her father years ago.

"You are so lucky and ahead of the game, Andrea. Just think if you had to work, darling. All you have to do is stay in school."

She interrupted Lorraine with, "Is my father there? Are you two just gonna play this game out until I give up?"

Her head was pounding with anger. A tear ran down her cheek as she faced the fact that she might not ever get home again, and back to her old life.

Without letting her voice quiver, she strongly said, "Okay, you're right, I'm lucky, Lorraine! Goodbye." She slammed the receiver of the pay phone down as hard as she could, making it echo throughout the hall.

That night, she cried herself to sleep.

· 2 ·

EVAN

A few weeks had passed, but nothing changed for Andrea. A heaviness cloaked her like a luxurious fur coat. She tried to cope with the feeling of no longer being special, known, or cared about. When she passed other students going to and from class, they didn't give her a second look. The reality that she might have to make new friends other than LaTrice and start a new life began to settle hard on her. She was out of plans and ideas to get back home. She was consumed with thoughts of doing something drastic that would get her out of Boston and back to New Jersey, but the perfect foolproof plan hadn't come yet.

Day after day, she went to class, the dining hall, and back to her room. Occasionally, Andrea would visit LaTrice in the evening while she dressed up to be wined and dined by a new man she had met here or there.

On her way to eat at the Murphy Dining Hall, she thought again about her situation. She was feeling more and more depressed by the day, but she knew she couldn't go crazy. She was too strong for that. She had to find a way, that's all, a way home!

Murphy Hall was a short walk from her dorm. It was named for a wealthy businesswoman who was a BU alumnus who had donated a lot of money to the school. Most students called it the "Murph". The students joked that, if you ate there, something would go wrong. It was a typical college campus cafeteria where the students complained about the food. Andrea always ate alone, sitting at the same table in the corner next to the old-fashioned jukebox that played modern music, complete with flashing lights all around it. It was placed in the Murph to raise student morale. But people didn't hang out there long enough to feed it quarters; they took the party to a dorm room or elsewhere.

Before Andrea knew it, she was already sitting at her corner table with her dinner tray. She didn't remember the walk, entering the Murph, or sliding her tray along the metal rails and picking out her food.

She was eating her mac and cheese in such a daze that she never saw a guy put a quarter in the flashing jukebox until his selection started playing. The guy walked back to his table across from hers and sat down in front of his tray. She stared at him until he looked up and met her gaze. He was a light-skinned black guy with black thick curls that needed a haircut. He was husky and only about five foot ten. Quickly assessing him, she decided he was a college student and not worth a flirting smile. He kept looking at her as if he wanted to say something, but they were too far away from each other. Andrea looked away from him and his curls and continued to eat her dinner. The next thing she knew, he was standing over her with his tray asking if he could sit down. She was shocked by his boldness, since she gave him no indication that she was interested during their stare-down.

"Can I sit?" he asked.

"Umm, sure, I guess," she answered waving her fork towards the seat across from her with no interest.

He placed his tray down and sat where she directed him with her fork. He reached across the table with his hand stuck out.

"Hi, I'm Evan."

She reached toward him and shook his hand stiffly. She wasn't feeling good about the introduction.

"Hi, I'm Andrea," she said blandly.

"Hi, Andrea. I've seen you here a few times. Freshman?"

"Yup, how can you tell?"

"I don't know; you have that lost look," he chuckled.

"Nope, not lost, just new," she answered his observation.

"Welcome to BU. What's your major? Where you from? What dorm are you in?" he spouted with his mouth full before she could answer his first question.

"New Jersey."

"Okay, okay," he nodded. "You're a Jersey Girl, huh? I heard about y'all!"

"What do you mean you heard about us?" She grinned, warming up a bit.

"Nah, I'm just kiddin'. Jersey Girls are cool, just high maintenance and all. But I'll give it to Jersey; some fine girls come from the Garden State!"

They shared the laugh about New Jersey, and the tension floated away. They ate and talked about campus life and the bad food. Since

Evan was from Boston, he told her about places to go and things to do. He mentioned that he was studying to be a lawyer and planned to stay in Boston after he graduated in a few months. He hoped to start his own law firm. Andrea avoided talking about her future because she didn't have any plans, hopes, or dreams that had to do with Boston University.

He continued to rattle on about his future, his family, and his love for the law. They were still sitting, talking and getting to know each other after the cafeteria had closed. The display food warmers had been dismantled, and the floor had been mopped around them. Lights were being shut off one at a time.

"I guess we better get out of here before they lock us in," Andrea said.

"Wow, I lost track of time," Evan answered while looking at his watch.

They took their trays to the trash slowly while they sorted out where each other's dorms were.

Once outside the Murph's locked doors, they stood for an hour talking.

"It was really nice to meet you, Andrea Moore."

"Yeah, it was nice to meet you too, Evan Livingston," she said sarcastically. "Maybe I'll see you here again, and we can share a table," she offered.

"Cool, well, have a good night," he said while walking away slowly with his hands in his front jean pockets.

She stood there for a moment and watched him walk away. She tried not to enjoy their encounter, but she had. For a few hours, she had forgotten about her problems and listened to someone who was very happy about his life. His conversation wasn't about trying to impress her or put on a whole act to hook up with her that night or a night in the near future. He was just a guy who met a girl and shared a piece of himself with no expectations from her. She liked that.

As she started to walk back to her dorm, she folded her arms around herself to lock out a chill that was in the air. Just then, she noticed that she had on BU sweatpants and a BU sweatshirt! She was so caught up in Evan's conversation that she hadn't remembered that she was slumming in college wear.

"Oh, God!" she said out loud to herself.

She continued her path to her dorm with her ponytail swinging left to right behind her head.

A night of studying was waiting for her when she reached her room so she set up her desk, pulled out her psychology books, and got to it. Every time the pay phone rang in the hallway, she cracked the door to hear who it was for, hoping it was her father calling for her; but it never was. She tried to get focused to study, but something was breaking her concentration. It wasn't the pay phone; it was Evan.

He really piqued her interest. It was more than the fact that he wasn't trying to date her. Something about him stayed on her mind. She tried to figure out what it was. He had told her about his parents and how they couldn't afford to send him to college and how he worked so hard to keep himself there, getting all the loans and scholarships he could. He explained how his parents couldn't support him monetarily but that they supported him in every other way and were very proud of him. She really felt the love he had for his parents.

Her mind wondered further, trying to guess if Evan had a girlfriend and how she would feel about him inviting himself to eat with other girls on campus. Andrea thought so hard about Evan and his intentions that she had nothing left for psychology. The desk and the books eventually found her head on them asleep.

The next night, LaTrice was in a panic because at the last minute she was invited to a white party and only had a white skirt and no white top to match it. Standing in Andrea's room, she told her the dilemma and said she had no time to get to a mall.

"Do you have anything, girl, for me to borrow? This was last minute, and I don't want to miss this party. My guy is a very important man in Boston, and it will be very beneficial for me to meet some of the people he knows."

Andrea reluctantly whipped open her closet door and started moving around shirts and blouses in the white section of her color-coordinated wardrobe. LaTrice was shocked that Andrea had such a high quality wardrobe. She didn't let it show, but she thought that the nice jewelry Andrea wore were gifts and had no idea that she had the money or the taste to have designer labels in her closet.

Andrea pulled out a white sweater, two white blouses, and a white V-neck vest and laid them on the bed.

"Girl, look at these! I'll take this Dior blouse," LaTrice squealed.

"Take it and have a good time!"

"Thanks, girl. I'll have it dry cleaned," she said as she ran out of the door.

The next few days were better for Andrea. She was still working on the big plan but made room to think about Evan. She kept her eyes peeled around campus for him but didn't see him. She made sure she pulled out of her slump enough to wear her designer jeans, leather boots, and one of her Tommy Hilfiger, Polo, or Liz Claiborne sweaters to class. She made sure the next time she saw Evan she wouldn't be in sweats.

LaTrice returned the next week to Andrea's room with her Dior blouse hung in the dry cleaner's plastic wrap. She thanked her for letting her wear it and sat down to tell her all about the white party and the important man she escorted to the event but didn't get but two sentences in before a bang came to the door.

"Andrea... phone!" the voice screamed from the other side. Before LaTrice could excuse herself, Andrea was out the door and down the hall to the dangling receiver.

"Hello," she said, out of breath.

"Is this Andrea, Andrea Moore?"

With a disappointing sigh, she answered, "Yes, who's this?"

"Hey, its Evan. Remember me, from the Murph?"

"Oh, yeah. Hi, Evan. How did you get this number?"

"You told me which dorm you lived in, and there is a directory of every pay phone on campus. Didn't you get one?"

"Well, you found me." She had a smile on her face now. She relaxed into the call, setting aside her disappointment that it wasn't her father.

"Do you have a room phone that I can call you back on?"

"No, I've been meaning to have one put in but just haven't been able to get to it."

"I see, you are a busy lady. Well, since you are standing in a hallway, I'll make it quick." He started to stumble over his words. "Do you wanna go out tonight? I mean maybe get something to eat? Oh, and not at the Murph. Like real food?"

Her mind rolled over the idea during a silent pause trying to find a reason not to, but she couldn't come up with a reason, so she said yes.

"Great, I'll come to get you in an hour. Does that work for you?"

"Sure, I'll be ready. I'll meet you out front."

She did a mad dash around her room, pulling out clothes like LaTrice did for her last minute date the week before. She decided on a Gianni Versace multicolored wrap dress that accentuated her bust and laid on her body like the expensive dress it was. She put on tall heels and a two-inch-thick 24-karat gold herringbone necklace. A few squirts of Fendi perfume, and she was almost ready. She didn't have time to wash and straighten her hair, so she wet it and slicked it into a bun on the back of her neck. She hadn't dressed up in so long that she enjoyed the process and walked out of the building like Andrea from New Jersey. She welcomed her old self back, tossing Andrea from Boston aside for a night.

Standing on the sidewalk in front of the dorm, she was getting all kinds of attention, which she ignored because she was used to it. She did think that it was funny how she had been there all this time, and, while she did get looks from guys, she didn't get what she was getting now.

She couldn't wait to get across the table from Evan and hear about his plans for that week. He seemed like the kind of guy who could get excited about anything and had all sorts of opinions about everything. She enjoyed his energy, and being in his presence changed her energy and she knew that was good.

After five minutes of standing there, a car pulled up right in front of her, and Evan got out. As he approached her, she tried not to show her distress. Then he stood in front of her, trying not to show his own distress. He was wearing blue jeans, sneakers, and a BU sweatshirt and still needed a haircut. Parked next to him was an old Chevy Chevette that looked as if, had she not seen it pull up, it couldn't actually move. He saw a woman he has never seen before waiting for him. The woman he had dinner with at the Murph was shy and sweet and a great listener who needed a friend. She was a down to earth girl who seemed to be perfect for him. *Who is this?* He thought! Her face was the same, but the dollar signs all over her shocked and scared him.

"Hey, Andrea. Wow! You look, Wow!"

"Thanks. Ahhh, this is your car, huh?"

"Yup, and you look like you are wearing more than the car is worth."

He rushed around to the trunk, opened it, and pulled out a beach towel. He then opened the passenger's side door for her and laid the beach towel across the seat for her to sit on. Andrea slowly stepped toward the open door and gently sat in the tiny car that smelled like old cracking vinyl and motor oil. Evan gently closed the door after she was in on the clean towel. He ran around to the driver's side and hopped in.

He looked down, closed his eyes, and then turned to her, saying, "Look, I didn't mean for you to get all dressed up. I'm a dude on a budget, remember? I was just gonna take you to a pizza spot. I had such a nice time talking with you before, and I couldn't wait to see you again. I think, well, I thought you were in the same position I was in, just trying to survive here. I won't hold it against you if you don't wanna go now. I'm sorry."

"Evan, look it's my fault. I misunderstood. I came because I wanted to see you again too. I didn't do much talking when we met, but I enjoyed getting to know you, and you were right about me. I am trying to survive here too, just not in the same way you are. I do want to have pizza with you. Let's go."

Evan felt an intimidation he didn't feel when he first laid eyes on her and he was now rethinking everything he had said to her. She was so beautiful, and he felt like a dummy for judging her look and not allowing her to talk about herself.

They pulled up in front of a pizza shop, and he ran around the car to open the door for her. He grabbed her delicate hand and pulled her out of his old beat up car the most stunning woman he ever seen. He was embarrassed but had to go through with it. They found a cozy semi-circled booth inside with the predictable clichéd decor of an Italian pizza shop. She looked at the green and red stripes and all the pictures of Italy on the walls and chuckled. She was looking for his excitement about life and enthusiastic conversation, but he was quiet and unsettled. Andrea took the band out of her bun and let her now crinkled hair fall from the bun in a half-dried, half-wet mess. She wiped her lipstick off, kicked off her heels under the table, and curled her legs to the side on the seat. She leaned into him, saying, "I like you, Evan, and this is fine."

He relaxed and dished their slices of pizza from the pie in the center of the table. Before long, he was talkative and animated the way she expected and wanted. This time, he asked her questions in an attempt to get to know her. She talked about her hometown, her friends, and her summers down the shore. She talked in the same excited way he did but about all-day beach trips in Jersey, baking in the sun on a blanket with a cooler full of sodas and snacks. She described boardwalk food and told him it was the best at the Jersey shore. Italian sausage sandwiches, cannolis, and funnel cakes were among her favorites. She laughed at how her mom would move the beach umbrella a million times as the sun moved to shield them from the rays, but it never worked. She explained that you couldn't leave the shore without trying to build a sandcastle or collecting seashells. They laughed together when she told the story of how a strong wave took her swimsuit top out to sea and left her topless. She didn't mention that at her house they had a pool, a housekeeper, and memberships to an exclusive country club in town. What she didn't realize was that Evan didn't have to hear that from her lips to know that she came from money. He also knew she wasn't mentioning it for a reason. He saw in her a girl who was looking for love, the kind of love money couldn't buy. His idea of her was based on who she presented at the Murph, but he was very wrong. Andrea wanted what Evan had, an enthusiasm for life. She thought that maybe by being around him it would rub off on her. If it didn't, she could at least bask in it whenever she was in his presence. She reasoned that, while she was trying to figure out what to do with her life, she could be with him, even though he didn't have anything to give her and couldn't even afford a decent dinner. She could deal with that for now she thought. At the same time, Evan was trying to convince himself also that this could work, that he was enough for her because she was there with him despite his small beginnings.

He pulled up in front of her dorm and walked around the car to open the door for her again. She took his hand and stepped out onto the sidewalk. He closed the door and then faced her, messy hair and all.

"Thank you for tonight," he said, "Ah…I mean, for making me feel comfortable. I'm glad I met you in sweats first. This, I mean all of this is just a bonus. You're beautiful inside and out, Andrea."

He leaned in to kiss her, and she accepted. Once their lips met, it was better than they both expected, so they embraced without unlocking their lips. She felt their connection run through her body. When they gently pulled away, not a word was spoken. They just stared at each other.

Evan broke the silence. "Let me walk you to the door. Come on." She followed slightly behind with her hand locked with his. Once at the door, she quickly pecked him on the lips and rushed inside after punching in the security code. She purposely didn't look back. Her heart spoke and asked, *what was that?* She didn't dare try to answer the question. She pushed it away.

Over the next few weeks, Andrea's mood changed completely. She was seeing Evan as often as possible and spent lots of time just talking about his future and his plans. She was surprised that she felt herself falling for him and knew that was a problem. But he touched her somewhere she didn't know was possible. Now when he took her out for a bite to eat, she wore jeans, a fresh face, and a plain T-shirt or sweater. They were quite a pair, and he was helping her through her stay at BU. She was keeping up with her classes and meeting a few more people who lived in her dorm. She hadn't forgotten her master plan, but for now she was enjoying Evan.

· 3 ·

THE DATE

A knock at the door startled Andrea out of a daydream about homecoming in a few weeks. She knew she wouldn't be going home until then.

"Who is it?"

A voice came back through the door, "Phone!"

She didn't run like she use to when she expected her father to be on the other end. She now hoped it would be Evan. Reaching the pay phone at the end of the hall, she answered, "Hello?"

"Dirty Girl, what you doing, huh?"

"LaTrice, why are you calling me on the pay phone when we're just down the hall from each other?"

31

"Look, my dude is here! He's here in Boston. Right downtown at the Grand Mirage. He's here on business, and he's ready to spoil me. His man is with him, so you know what that means, right?"

"His man, what? Like…… is he bisexual? He got you and a man?"

"No, Dirty Girl, his boy, his friend, his partner!"

"Look, you got one more, Dirty Girl, and it's gonna be on!" Andrea shot at LaTrice.

"You know I'm just kiddin'. You're my girl, my fellow label whore!"

"I'm your girl like your boyfriend has a man?" Andrea responded. They both gave a halfhearted chuckle. Before Andrea could hang up on Latrice. LaTrice popped her head out of her dorm room and yelled to Andrea to come to her room. Reluctantly, Andrea swept down toward LaTrice's room, dragging her slippered feet.

LaTrice's room was decked out like a modern New York City apartment. She was in her black satin lounge outfit pouring champagne while pitching what she was selling. Andrea took the champagne flute and indulged.

"Listen, we've run into a problem," LaTrice stated.

Andrea took a sip from her flute and shivered as the bubbles tickled her nose before asking, "What kind of problem?"

"My man Rodrick is downtown like I said with his boy. They are doing business here. The date I had for his partner didn't come through, so now he's like a third wheel. Can you help us out? Please? We need to show him a good time. It will be a nice dinner out, and he won't be bored sitting up there with us if you come."

"I know you are excited to see your boyfriend but I'm gonna pass. I really need to study tonight, and I don't need any more distractions. By the looks of things, if I don't hit these books, I won't have anywhere to go. My parents have kicked me to the curb."

LaTrice, looking like a sneaky cat, leaned back in her chair, still holding her champagne, and said, "Well, looks like you need to do for yourself to have the life you want. If you play your cards right, you could have a much easier time here. This guy who runs with my man doesn't have a girl. I'm sure he would treat you like Rod treats me when he comes to town. You need a sponsor to keep up the lifestyle you are accustomed to that you no longer have, girlfriend. When was the last time you were over at the Diamond Hills Mall purchasing a designer dress?"

Andrea wondered why LaTrice kept thinking that she was broke. Her problem wasn't money as long as she stayed in Boston.

"LaTrice, it just sounds like you are prostituting yourself out for things. I mean, really, how important is your boyfriend when you've been seeing so many other men for stuff?"

"Let me fix your mind on this thing, girl," LaTrice said in a snarly tone. "I do what I need to do. I am my top priority. I have what it takes to keep a man or a few men who treat me like the queen I am. If it looks like I'm getting a little dirty in the process, don't judge. Look at the end results."

LaTrice then gestured to all the luxuries around her college dorm room. Her eyes focused back on Andrea.

"I call you Dirty Girl because you have her in you. You come off like the sweet innocent cheerleader, but I see what you're really about. You will push that sadness you have aside when you have to and do what you naturally have in you to do in order to have what you want." Taking another sip from her glass, LaTrice casually said, "We are going to the Diamond Hills Mall 'cause I need to get those designer dresses that he promised; then we are going to dinner at Von Meres. You don't have to give it up; he just needs a dinner companion. You can get all dressed up, put on your best jewelry, and get treated like a lady should

34

with dinner at a real restaurant. He just wants to take a nice girl to dinner, that's all. I'm in a jam."

Andrea put her glass down. "Well, that's nice, but I'm busy tonight." She stood up and thanked LaTrice for the champagne.

On her way back to her room, she tried to comprehend every word LaTrice said about her really being a Dirty Girl. She noticed that LaTrice's accent was nowhere to be found in that conversation.

She got to her door and found a sticky note on it with a phone message that read:

Phone call from: Evan
Tacos tonight! Meet me out front at
7:00 pm. Wear your BU sweatshirt.
I'm wearing mine!

While crumpling the sticky note up, she went to the pay phone to call him back but got his answering machine. So she left a message.

"Hi, it's Andrea. I'm sorry I can't make it tonight. I have a ton of homework, and I need to study for a test I gotta take tomorrow. Rain check on the tacos? Talk to you tomorrow. Bye."

She dialed another number with her calling card.

LaTrice picked up. "Hello?"

"What time?"

"Oh thank you! 7 pm out front girl."

Andrea put the phone back on the hook and headed back to her room unsure that she was making the right decision. She knew she was only going to have a night out at a fancy restaurant but questioned if that made her as bad as LaTrice even though she had no intentions of shopping or sleeping with this guy.

She felt good knowing she could get dressed and give it her all because these guys were taking them to Von Meres. This was the real deal. No pizza, tacos, or burgers tonight. She started the dressing ritual and got happier the closer she got to looking like Andrea from New Jersey. The makeup had to be perfect, and her hair got rolled and set for this mystery date. A designer dress was pulled from the closet and diamonds set out from her portable safe that was hidden in the wall.

On her first day, she had cut out a space in the wall for her safe and then put the drywall back in the cut-out space. A picture hung over it and was undetectable to anyone looking to rob her.

When she was done dressing, she saw in the full length mirror every bit of how she wanted to look. Her hair was flowing in big smooth sleek curls lying on the shoulders of her silk Chanel dress. She wore her favorite diamond tennis bracelet and a smaller version of it around her ankle. She sashayed on three inch Via Spiga pumps. Her already

36

long and lush eyelashes were coated with midnight colored mascara taking them up to extra sexy. Her lips were painted a deep burgundy, which matched her silk dress. As Andrea locked her door behind her, LaTrice was coming down the hall in equally impressive designer attire.

"You clean up nice, Dirty Girl!"

"Shut up, LaTrice!"

The two looked more like they were coming out of an upscale boutique in Manhattan than a college dorm.

A limousine with blackout tinted windows had arrived at 6:45 pm and was waiting out front, looking like it was in the wrong place. Students were passing it pointing and staring. It was not fully dark outside yet, so everyone was easily seen gawking.

Andrea and LaTrice walked out at exactly 7:00 pm looking like superstars and were received as such. Standing outside the limousine was LaTrice's boyfriend Rodrick, a handsome man, and the limousine driver who opened the door for them. The two gentlemen allowed the ladies in first before getting back inside themselves. The door was shut by the driver.

Pulling up just as Andrea was being helped into the limousine was Evan! He saw her, his new pretty thing being put into a limousine by the hand of a man. He couldn't believe what he was seeing and couldn't believe he misjudged her. He drove by quickly hoping not to be seen in his old junk car, and he wasn't.

Once inside the long car, LaTrice introduced Rodrick to Andrea, and Rodrick introduced his business partner to both ladies as Easton Graham. To Andrea's surprise, LaTrice was meeting Easton for the first time too. The Jamaican accents were flying everywhere. LaTrice fell back into hers very heavily. Easton reached out and clasped Andrea's hand with both of his and then kissed it, leaning across the limo practically on his one knee. It felt strange to her.

"I did not expect you to be so beautiful. I appreciate you coming tonight," he said while still holding her hand. His accent wasn't as thick when he was complimenting her. He sounded like he had been in the U.S. for a long time and had just a twinge of an accent except when he was speaking to Rodrick and LaTrice. She wondered why they did that, turned it on and off.

Andrea graciously accepted his hand kiss and replied, "It's nice to meet you too," with a tilted head.

Easton was tall, a man of twenty-six with smooth dark skin and dark Asian-shaped smoldering eyes that smiled before his mouth did.

His teeth were perfect and the whitest of whites. He was almost six feet with a slim but muscular build. His hair was midnight black with shiny waves. Everything about him said smooth. He had on an expensive tailored dark charcoal grey suit with no tie and his shirt open by one button.

LaTrice and Rodrick started to shuffle around in the limo changing places. Easton followed their lead and moved next to Andrea so Rodrick and LaTrice could sit together.

Rodrick was good looking as well, in a black suit that definitely wasn't off the rack. He was a nice brown skinned man with a low haircut and on the slight side. He didn't really look natural with LaTrice, Andrea thought, but her attention moved back to her date, Easton.

"I promise you a great night, Andrea," Easton said while he moved his face daringly close to hers.

LaTrice and Rodrick were speaking soft and gentle to each other in the far corner of the car. They had a private moment going on between people with plans.

The limo slowly pulled away to the beat of Reggae music being played by the driver who also had a Jamaican accent. The ride was smooth and very cozy. Watching people stare and wonder who was inside the limousine was entertaining to LaTrice but unsettling to Andrea.

They pulled in front of the Diamond Hills Mall and got out. The people gathering to see who was inside of the limo made Andrea feel uncomfortable, so she went back inside the car and told Easton she would wait there, since they would only be an hour. He waved Rodrick and LaTrice on and got back inside the car with her.

"I wanted to buy you something," Easton said.

"Why? I just met you."

"Oh," he said looking shocked. "I thought…"Then he stopped and looked at her.

"What, you thought what?" she questioned.

He quickly backed off his comment.

"I just wanted to show you how grateful I am that you came out tonight. I'm sure you have other things you could be doing."

"I thought I was having dinner with a nice guy my friend thought I would like," she assured him.

"Yes, yes, thank you, but I think I am the winner here. You are so beautiful, and you seem very sweet. I can see it all over you."

That made her fight back a smile. In the comfort of the limousine, she asked him all kinds of questions for which he seemed to have ready answers. The conversation flowed like it should between two people attracted to each other and meeting for the first time. He was making a big effort to impress her and say all the right things. He told her he had several successful stores around Jamaica and that he'd been fortunate the last few years that business was good. He explained that, because of that, he was able to come to the U.S. to make deals for merchandise and also have some fun in between.

"I expected to be a hanger on with those two tonight, but wow I got lucky to share the night with you. Tell me about you," he said and placed his hand on the top of her leg. She gave a surprised look, so he drew back his hand quickly. She spotted a gold bracelet on his wrist with diamonds set in the links as his hand drew back. The sparkle it made on the ceiling of the car took her attention from the touch. She told him about her parents and life in suburban Scotch Plains. Of course, this was completely different from growing up in Jamaica and being a self-made man. All the things Easton could afford could not give him the experience of growing up in suburban America. Her expensive look seemed not to match the sheltered small-town

41

upbringing she was describing to him, yet she seemed savvy enough to be where she is right now, he thought.

When LaTrice and Rodrick came back to the car with more shopping bags than the driver could fit in the truck, it broke up the intimate private time they were both enjoying. LaTrice and Rodrick exuded an element of greed that didn't exist in the space of Andrea and Easton. More talk of buying expensive things made Andrea again feel very uncomfortable.

Von Meres was an elegant, dark, and modern restaurant with silver fixtures and water falling everywhere like a rain forest. Of course, it was the kind of place where the ladies' menus did not have prices. Easton ordered the wine, and it seemed as though the staff knew him. Andrea felt she could order the lobster without worrying about sending some poor college kid to the back to wash dishes. She pointed to Lobster Newburg on the menu. Easton nodded and ordered for her when the waiter came to the exquisitely set table. In the fashion of posh restaurants, the food portions were small and barely enough, but the atmosphere was wonderful. Andrea felt special and well treated.

The conversation was light, and Andrea was able to talk to Easton uninterrupted because Rodrick and LaTrice were in their own world. She now knew why LaTrice needed Easton occupied because they intended to be coupled up all night. Easton spoke of things that thrilled Andrea like the beaches in Jamaica, the expensive places he had been in the States, and the kinds of luxury items he liked to buy. He wasn't trying to be someone, she thought. He already was someone, and he wasn't four years away from making his own money. He already had it.

After the long dinner was over, they walked outside around the amazing grounds of the restaurant, which was a part of the dinner experience at Von Meres. Bushes and trees were cut and carved into animal shapes inside a massive shrub maze created for walking through like an outdoor museum. There were also large stone sculptures inside the maze. Warm glowing fire pits were strategically placed near stone benches for lovers to enjoy the crisp night air in the moonlight. Andrea and Easton stood together at the beginning of the path taking in the cool air.

"Where's your dreads, Mr. Rasta Man?" she joked. He rubbed his head in the direction of the waves in his black shiny hair while smiling.

"Yah, I had dem gal, but yu know bein' a business mon an all, mi needin' to be short and wavy like yu Americans do."

That made her laugh because she never expected him to have a sense of humor. He was becoming the complete package to her.

LaTrice and Rodrick wondered off in a different direction. Andrea and Easton were still standing next to each other, her arms folded across herself holding her purse close to her body not sure what to do next. Her folded arms signified to him that she might be cold. He took his suit jacket off and put it over her shoulders. Her folded arms were because she didn't know where else to put them, but the outcome was okay with her. The smell of his rich cologne greeted her sweetly up close from his jacket. She could feel the weight of his belongings on the inside chest pocket. *What does he have in there?* she thought. He's not driving; it can't be keys. She didn't feel it with her hand as she was tempted to do. She just kept enjoying the smell of him and the warmth of his jacket even though she wasn't cold. He moved in close, put his arm around her, and guided her towards one area after another on the beautiful property.

They walked and talked and let the feeling of newness settle on them. She talked about Boston and all the things it had to offer for visitors, which she had learned from Evan. He spoke about how the service back at the Grand Mirage Hotel was more than he could ask for. He told her about the most popular resorts in Jamaica that drew the tourists. He explained that most vacationers flew into Montego Bay, better known as "Mo'Bay," and went by buses to the many resorts on that side of the island. He told her how much he loved living in his tropical country where the culture was so rich. He spoke of his beachfront home where he leaves his bedroom windows open at night so he can hear the waves lap on the beach. It all seemed so magical to her. *Could he be for real? He's so handsome, charming, and already established,* she said to herself. He realized that she wasn't in this like LaTrice but couldn't believe she wasn't in it for something. When Rodrick told him that they had to replace the other girl for the night, he didn't know it was with a girl who had no clue. He knew when he touched her leg and when she didn't want to shop that she was not a part of the deal and that he wouldn't be having sex with her that night. In her mind, she was really just on a date with a guy her friend set her up with. It was kind of nice for him to have something so normal and above board, so he stayed in the moment and enjoyed it.

That night, Andrea laid comfortably in bed with a scrubbed face and body now free from her designer dress and the three-inch heels. She thought of the night and how different it was from the dates with guys back home and her quarterback. She was used to nice restaurants and certainly being treated well, but this was different. Easton was a grown man with his own business and clearly didn't need her to jump onboard to some dream he had. She turned over to her side sleep position thinking of the gentle kiss he put on her lips at the door. LaTrice was still in the car and was going back to the hotel with them to spend the night with Rodrick. While they exchanged pleasant goodnights, she hoped he would kiss her, just so she'd know, in case she never saw him again, what it was like. It felt sweet, secure, strong, and romantic all rolled up into one. She took his suit jacket from around her shoulders slowly trying to get a deep sniff to remember the smell of him. He was in charge and able to keep it that way. Tonight no tears, fears or worries for her, just peaceful sleep.

· 4 ·

AFTER

The next day, as Andrea walked up to her dorm room door from English Lit., there on the hall floor in front of it were a dozen yellow roses displayed in the most beautiful arrangement in a crystal vase. She knew immediately who they were from. She looked around, hoping he wasn't coming down the hall or hiding around a corner in his finely tailored suit while she stood there in jeans with her hair in its natural curly state, ponytailed with several wayward curls that escaped the scrunchy hair tie. He wasn't in sight, so she quickly grabbed her roses and got the key in the door. Once in, she helped the door close faster behind her and clicked the lock. She pulled the card from the flowers and smelled one of the roses first. She flopped on her bed smiling, with the card in her hand.

Andrea,

I knew the moment I touched your leg it would not be the last time I saw you. I hope I was correct.

Thank you for a memorable evening. Please give me the pleasure again.

Warmly,
East

She made her way down the hall to LaTrice's room, hoping she was there. LaTrice opened the door and let a rushing Andrea in. Andrea showed her the card and began asking her a million questions about Easton.

"Hold up. I don't know much about him except that him and Rod work together. They come here to buy merchandise for their stores back home. I met him once before at a club with Rod in Kingston."

Andrea immediately thought that was strange since Rodrick introduced them both to Easton. Maybe Rodrick didn't realize that LaTrice had met him once before, Andrea thought, especially since they were all wrapped up together like they were the night before.

LaTrice continued, "Rod never talks about him, so I guess he's just one of the dudes trying to get paper. That's all I know. You like him, right?"

"LaTrice, he's real smooth, mature, and so fine!"

"The money don't hurt either, huh girl?"

LaTrice pulled out a cigarette, lit it, and blew the smoke out like a pro.

"You smoke? Since when?"

"I smoke every now and then."

"Wow, I didn't know that."

"There's lots you don't know *'bout me, gal.*" LaTrice continued with, "So tonight I'm going to the hotel. You want to hang out? We are getting something to eat and watching a movie in the suite. You know that new movie that everyone's talking about, 'Ghost' ? I told Rod to get it for me."

"Wait, isn't that in the theaters now?" Andrea asked.

"There are no limits to what I want and to what Rod can make happen for me. While he's here, his job is to keep me happy in every way. He got the movie on VHS."

"The night sounds really relaxed and easy. Will you ask him if I can come with you?"

She flicked her cigarette into a silver ashtray and said, "Don't worry, I'm sure he's okay with it."

Not wanting to make the same mistake being overdressed for just a movie, she thought she'd ask LaTrice what to wear. "Should I wear jeans and…?"

Cutting her off, LaTrice said, "Ahh No! Don't get comfortable, girl. Do you know the choices he has? You got lucky, the girl who was supposed to meet him wasn't able to go. Just follow my lead with these guys. You need to stay on top of your game in order to catch this fish."

"Really? So we are going to sit around dressed up?" Andrea questioned.

Taking another pull from her cigarette, LaTrice responded, "Yup. Don't ever slip because the next chick won't. You want to be comfortable, get naked!" They both laughed at what Andrea took for a joke.

"Girl, you are a mess. Let me know when I should be ready." As Andrea headed towards LaTrice's door, she noticed that besides the shopping bags still unpacked from the night before she had boxes of china by Lenox with place settings inside, crystal stemware, a goose down comforter, and a cappuccino maker all lined against the wall. She stopped her departure and said, "Hey, when did you get all this new stuff?"

"I had it picked out and just needed Rod to pay for it and had it delivered this morning. I'm hoping that on his next visit I will be moving from this dorm into a nice apartment. But baby steps for now. I have to keep him interested so he will come back and take care of me the right way!"

Andrea couldn't spend any time trying to figure out LaTrice and what she was up to. She wanted to only think about Easton, so she kept moving towards the door so she could get to her next class.

· 5 ·

THE GRAND MIRAGE

Andrea had music pumping in her room as she danced and got dressed up for her movie night with Easton. She chose a pair of black dressy Palazzo pants with a matching white blouse made of the same fabric. She belted the outfit with a gold multilayered chain belt that dripped with imitation European coins. At her neck, she had a long layered necklace that was similar to the belt. She slipped into satin Stuart Weitzman pumps that you couldn't see unless she was walking because the pants covered the shoes, almost hitting the ground. She made sure her hair was clean, dry, blown straight and pulled into a high ponytail with curls at the ends. Her lips were painted blood red and her eyes darkened with heavy black eyeliner and mascara. Over the loud music, she heard a knock at her door. It was LaTrice dressed to the nines.

"Let's go, Dirty Girl. The limo's here."

"Stop calling me that, dammit!"

LaTrice gave her a smirk and said, "Umm…humm, whatever."

It was dark outside, and, just like before, the guys plus the driver were standing outside the car waiting. Easton looked so good. His white teeth shining through the darkness is what she saw first. His voice called to her before she arrived at his side. He hugged her and gave her a look like she was a cupcake at a kid's party all whipped up and pretty. The guys were in dress pants, buttoned-up silk shirts, and leather shoes, which Andrea thought looked Italian. Both men had on tailored sports jackets that nicely completed their look. The routine was the same as the night before. LaTrice and Rodrick cuddled and whispered in the corner while Easton gazed at Andrea. The dark cabin of the car with padded fabric made it feel as if they were already in a cozy room and not traveling down the road in a limousine. Pulled close to him she felt the urge to lay her head on his shoulder. It felt like a natural thing to do, so she did. Easton held her tighter. It was an unspoken message asking him to take care of her that night, and

Andrea was sure he got the message. She told herself that she wanted whatever LaTrice and Rodrick appeared to have, but she wanted the feelings to be real.

The Grand Mirage in downtown Boston was magnificent, with lights circling the entire building. The limo pulled up in front, and this time the driver didn't exit. Instead, the door was opened by a hotel doorman who was dressed like a toy soldier. Easton exited first and held his hand out for Andrea who stepped out into the bright entrance of The Grand Mirage.

They stood aside and waited for LaTrice and Rodrick to exit the car too.

Once everyone was out and standing together, the limo drove off. Doors were held open repeatedly all the way into the lobby of the hotel. The marble floor echoed with the click of the ladies' heels. Exquisite chandeliers hung strategically throughout the lobby. Andrea noticed a group of formally dressed people gathering in front of a ballroom that had music pouring from its doors. She walked next to Easton with a regal stride like she belonged there, like she was his woman. She felt pretty and worthy of being by his side because he made her feel that way. It felt very right to her, and she couldn't get enough of the almost tangible power that surrounded him. As they passed the front desk, the female clerk uniformed in the same colors as the doormen said, "Have a good evening, Mr. Graham." Easton didn't respond; he just nodded at her. The four kept strolling past the front desk and down the hall to where the people who were milling around could no longer be seen and the music from the banquet could no longer be heard. It was quiet, and the décor made Andrea feel rich just being there.

When she went to luxury hotels with her father and Lorraine, she never noticed all the things that caught her eye here at the Mirage. She was always trying to escape from them to do her own thing and never stopped to admire anything. Andrea stood with the others in front of closed elevator doors waiting for one to return to the lobby after Rodrick pressed the gold call button. One elevator on the end binged, and the doors opened. They walked to the end car and entered. Soft music played inside the elevator as they looked at themselves in the wall-to-wall gold-trimmed mirrors. Easton pulled out a room key from the inside chest pocket of his sports coat and stuck it in the slot below the floor buttons. Once the card was recognized and a green light flashed, he pressed the 20th floor, which was at the very top.

"The penthouse, huh?" Andrea asked.

"Yah mon, di view is every ting ya know," Easton joked.

She laughed at his Jamaican accent and was surprised again that he could go in and out of it to be funny or talk with another Jamaican.

When they arrived at the penthouse, it was spectacular! Easton was right about the view. The far side of the suite was a wall of windows. The Boston skyline was a brilliant display of twinkling lights. Their penthouse had two bedrooms and a kitchen next to a dining area that folded into a living room. A game of dominos was set up on the dining table with no players. It seemed as though the game was not over and would be continued later.

Room service staff brought dinner to the room and placed it on the large glass coffee table in the living room near the TV. They had ordered finger foods like French fries, mozzarella sticks, crab cakes, BBQ ribs, and egg rolls along with several bottles of champagne. Buckets of popcorn were on the table for the movie also. Two large L-shaped overstuffed couches sat in front of the built-in mahogany entertainment center with a VCR tucked under the TV on a shelf. Each couple curled up at separate ends of the couch. As soon as the lights were down and LaTrice hit the play button on the remote, food was passed and champagne was poured. By the time Easton and Andrea had their third and fourth glasses of champagne, neither was paying attention to the movie. Each was thinking about how this night felt and where it would go next.

From the beginning, Easton had been checking his feelings, he kept checking to decide if what he felt about Andrea the minute they met was real. The second time he saw her, he felt the same chemistry, and he was sure she was the real deal. He refilled both their glasses again, and they clinked and raised them in a toast with no words before their sip. LaTrice and Rodrick snuck away to one of the suite's bedrooms and closed the door before the end of the movie.

Easton asked her, "Are you watching this?"

"No, not really. The champagne has me a little tipsy." He grabbed the remote and put the movie on pause.

"I'd much rather talk to you," he said.

"That's nice. What do you want to talk about, Mr. Graham?"

"I want to know where your boyfriend is tonight and how I can pay him to go away forever."

Andrea laughed while taking a sip from her glass, trying not to gush at the thought of Easton paying someone so he could have her. She liked the idea, and the alcohol was making it hard to hide that fact.

"I don't have one, a boyfriend," she stammered.

"I don't believe that for one second, Miss Moore. *A pretty gal like yu must be having a man now?*"

"Nope, I'm just trying to concentrate on the books." She elongated the "s" in in books.

"Wow, I must be *receivin'* a blessing from Jah to meet you with no boyfriend for me to get rid of."

They both laughed and continued to drink. Easton poured more champagne in both glasses, and they held them up to cheers again. Andrea tried to be cool and focus on the conversation but was having a hard time fighting the effects of all the champagne. She started to tell him more about how she ended up at Boston University and her love for clothes, shopping, and her friends who all went different directions after high school.

Easton was falling in love with her innocence. She was not like any other woman he had been with or met. Her naiveté posed a problem for him, but he would see where this was going before worrying about that. He wanted to spend money on her and give her all the things she spoke about that made her happy. They were very different, but they had a connection that he knew he wouldn't be able to forget about easily.

Now with her shoes off and her legs folded under her, Andrea continued talking about how hard it was adjusting to being away from home and how she wasn't motivated to make her home in Boston even though her father gave her a no-limit credit card to do whatever she wanted. Easton listened to every word trying to learn as much about her as possible. He knew she was tipsy and was talking freely. Andrea ran on and on about things that would bore any other date except Easton. He thought she was cute and that she was as pure as she seemed. Her sentences started to trail off, and her voice got quieter. Easton realized that she was beyond tipsy now. She drank way too much champagne. He took the glass from her hand and placed it on the coffee table next to the half-eaten appetizers.

"Did you get my flowers?"

She leaned over, half lying on him, and said, "Yes, I did. They are beautiful and such a nice thing to do. Thank you, East. Is that what people call you? East?"

"Yeah, they do, and I call myself East too." After a big sigh and a slow blink, she then said, "It's a nice name. I like it."

Easton was now mad at himself for letting her drink so much. He forgot she was under age. Her beautiful mature look, the expensive clothes, and the way she carried herself sober hid the 18-year-old girl she was. Her uncontrolled conversation led by the champagne made him even more enamored with her.

Easton scooped her up in his arms and carried her to his bedroom on the other side of the penthouse. She went easily, laughing with her eyes half open. She pulled the ponytail holder from her hair which now went wild, relieving the tension from her head that had been starting to pound. She still noticed, even through her haze, how expensive the drapes and bedding were. She said, "This is a really nice hotel; it's just like home. I mean my house isn't like a hotel. I mean my dorm is so ugly and drab like a mental institution. It's nice, the drapes."

Easton laid her down across his bed. Responding, he said, "It better be nice for what I'm paying to stay here for two weeks."

He kicked off his shoes, locked the door, and laid on the bed next to her. *She's so young and innocent*, he thought to himself. *Maybe I should rethink things.* He kissed her deeply. He had stirred up the passion between them. She followed him in the direction he wanted to go in every motion of their kissing and embrace. Then she settled, and in between each kiss, she randomly talked and chuckled. Each time he tried to go further, she said something cute that distracted him. "My God, East, this comforter is so soft. I feel like I'm on a cloud," she chuckled.

"I'll outfit your whole dorm room exactly like this room if you like it so much," he told her while kissing her neck.

"I can't let you do that," she answered.

"Then let me get you a condo near the school, and you can decorate it like this whole suite," he whispered.

She answered his offer without the perfect words she would have had if she were sober. "No, I'm not a whore, Easton!"

He stops his lips from moving across her face. He swept her hair from her eyes, held her face in his hands, and stared at her directly into her eyes as if he was searching for something. She blinked a few times and stared right back into his eyes. He moved very close to her face nose to nose and said, "What is this? What's happening here?"

Her champagne soaked mind couldn't put it together fast enough to respond. His mind began to take a different route than his body wanted to take. He realized he wanted her for more than one night, for more than just a few weeks. He didn't want to use her for sex or for a cover to help him stay in the United States. He could see she was worth more than that.

Andrea interrupted his thinking with, "Do what you came in here to do, East. She started to unbutton her white blouse.

He watched for a few seconds but then stopped her and whispered in her ear, "No, not tonight. I want you straight baby, not like this. With me and you, it's gonna be different." He then started to unbutton her blouse for her and gently took off her flowing pants. He stood up, took off his own clothes, and returned to the plush bed, pulling up the luxurious comforter over both of them, lying behind her, and spooning her. He said quietly, "This is our first night together, and it's how I want it."

The next morning, to Andrea's surprise, she was not in class but still luxuriating on the expensive bedding at The Grand Mirage. She remembered that the number one rule among her girlfriends was that you never let the sunlight catch you if you spend the night with a guy who is not your man! She had never been in this position before, but she knew the rules. Embarrassed, she got up and started looking for her clothes. She was caught in the act when the man she spent the night with came through the bedroom door fully dressed for the day and smelling like heaven. She stood there in her bra and panties frozen, as if he couldn't see her if she stood very still.

"You alright?" he asked her.

She started to move again. "Oh, yes. Where are my clothes?" She moved the sheets around trying to find her blouse and pants.

"Don't worry. I gave them to housekeeping to be dry cleaned and pressed. I also went to the boutique downstairs and picked out a dress you can wear. I figured a woman can't leave in the same clothes she was wearing last night. It's hanging in the closet. If you don't like it, I'll have them bring up a few other things. There's a fresh robe in the bathroom." He pointed to the bathroom that she hadn't noticed the night before when he carried her into the bedroom. "Go ahead, take a shower. Everything you need should be in there, and when you come out, will you have breakfast with me?"

She sat down on the bed and put her face in her hands with shame. Easton walked over and sat next to her and brushed her hair back with his hand to try and find her face. She leaned over and put her head on his chest and felt the smooth fabric of his silky white dress shirt.

With her eyes closed, she said, "Oh my God, I can't believe this happened. I'm so embarrassed. Can you close the door so they don't see me like this?"

He pulled her face up. "We didn't do anything. We slept. We just went to sleep. You were too out of it to leave, so I tucked you in."

After a long pause, she said, "I know East, I remember. I was drunk, but I knew what I was doing. I just didn't think I'd fall asleep and be here in the morning searching for my clothes like this."

Suddenly her posture straightened, she moved a curl from her face, and she said, "I meant it. I wanted you to do it." He released air from his mouth like he wished now it had happened. He quickly shook off his lovesick demeanor that snuck up on him. "Baby, not that way. I want you to invite me in the right way, with no doubt in your mind what you want. I want it to be intoxicating between us… with no help from Dom Pérignon."

Still feeling overwhelmed by the situation, Andrea looked away and said again, "Can you close the door?"

"Oh, they're not here. I made them get out this morning, so you could get yourself together without them seeing you. We have the whole penthouse to ourselves. This is my suite. You are my special guest, and I want you to be comfortable. They're gone, and our breakfast is on the way." He stood up, offering his hand, and she took it and stood next to him. They hugged, and his hand slid down to squeeze one of her butt cheeks. Andrea laughed seductively as she moved his hand. "You had your chance last night!" she shot at him.

She went to the bathroom and took a bubble bath instead of a shower for the first time since her parents had shipped her off to college. The dorms only had showers. She felt like a princess surrounded by mounds of bubbles. Wrapped in the white fluffy robe Easton showed her, she went out to the dining area. The dominos were no longer on the table. Just as he said, breakfast was served. They sat, ate, and talked as if they had made love the night before. It was so real, honest, and comfortable, and she felt close to him. She was no longer trying to control the conversation. Easton felt comfortable too. He was trying to figure out how to make this woman his.

Night after night for the next week, they met for dinner, driven in the limousine that got so much attention everywhere they went. LaTrice and Rodrick opted out. It was just the two of them. They continued to share with each other their likes and dislikes and stories about their lives. She didn't go back to his penthouse for the whole week. They just spent time together out and about around Boston. They went to the aquarium, walked a few historical parks, and even took in a play.

After a night out dancing at a popular club downtown, they sat in the limo parked in front of her dorm talking about how the sweat from dancing had dried and returned several times during the night. Their skin felt sticky and itchy from the cycle. He leaned over and kissed her neck, which turned into full-on spastic kissing that rocked the limo from side to side. She stopped and immediately looked for the driver. Without a word, Easton gave a look that the driver saw in the rearview mirror, and he pushed the button to bring the divider up. Andrea felt the spark that set off a fire! She wanted to resist but couldn't. She laid back under Easton's weight.

Every night that week, he had given her a goodnight kiss at the dorm door. Now, he could wait no longer. He was fully on top of her, and she was letting go. They were on their way to making this his night. Again and again, he whispered in her ear *"Drea, Drea."*

They breathed heavily, continuing to kiss. His hands unbuckled, unsnapped, and loosened her clothes and his. Once her bare stomach touched his bare skin, she realized this was it, in the back seat of a limo!

It was too much. She knew it wasn't right. Not there, not rushed, and not when she couldn't breathe in the hot limo.

"Wait, wait, not here, not like this," she said.

He sat her up slowly from the seat and got a hold of himself. "I'm sorry baby, we could go back to the hotel and take a hot shower," he offered.

But she cut him off, saying, "Not tonight."

They both buttoned up and put their clothes back together. Andrea opened the door to the limo and jumped out before the driver could get out and get the door for her. Before Easton could follow her, she was up the sidewalk and rushing through the dorm doors. Easton clenched his teeth, angry with himself for the way he handled things. He wasn't his usual smooth self. He felt like a teenage boy, out of control by groping her, and he felt embarrassed.

Lying in bed that night, Andrea thought about Easton. Soon his two weeks would be up. He was going home, and she would still be here. Her mind drifted back to the kissing in the back of the limo. She wanted him as badly as he wanted her. But then, she wondered… *What is the point of sleeping with him? That won't change my life. I've only known him for two weeks. The most I can hope for after that is a long-distance relationship, and even then, would he be loyal? Even on a trial basis with him, how would that work?* She didn't need his money, and she couldn't accept being treated like his private whore when he returned to the States every three months. He couldn't solve her immediate problem. Getting a condo while she still had to earn a degree to make her father happy wasn't the answer. She was glad she didn't give in and go back to his hotel for the hot shower.

· 6 ·

EVAN LIVINGSTON, ESQUIRE

Andrea went back to classes and the regular routine she'd had before

meeting Easton. *Life has to go on,* she told herself. Though her days and

nights were so much better and bearable with him in them for the past

two weeks, she knew he was going home soon. Her plan was to avoid

him completely until he left the United States. She ignored his calls.

While at the Murph eating her dinner, she wondered if LaTrice

would be sad when Rodrick left. She also wondered if LaTrice was

spending all her time at The Grand Mirage in the new suite Rodrick

had to get after Easton kicked him out so he and Andrea could stay

there. Andrea laughed to herself about the wasted money because she

never went back to the penthouse after that first night. She wondered

if LaTrice was out spending more of Rodrick's money before his wallet got on the plane back to Jamaica. She chuckled to herself at her own joke.

While thinking of LaTrice and Rodrick, she saw a familiar face coming towards her. She squinted as if that would make her vision clearer to be sure who it was. But, in a split second, Evan was standing right in front of her. "Hi, Andy," he said, standing with his hands in the pockets of his BU sweatshirt looking at her like she had some explaining to do.

"Hi, how are you, Evan?" He didn't answer her.

"Can I sit down?" he said instead.

"Sure, go ahead."

She pointed to the empty seat right next to her. He instead pulled the chair out that was further from her. She hadn't thought about Evan in more than two weeks or about how she would explain not returning his calls if she ran into him on campus. She was upset at herself for not figuring out what to say in this situation before it happened. She knew it was inevitable that she would run into him. She wondered if perhaps they could pick up where they left off but with the understanding that they would be friends while she continued to work her master plan of getting out of Boston and back to Scotch Plains.

Now, with his hands back in the pockets of his sweatshirt as he sat across from her, he began talking as if he had a lot on his mind. "I've been calling you, and you haven't called me back. Did you get my message to call me? It's been two weeks."

Andrea continued eating her dinner while Evan talked to minimize his emotional questioning, as if it wasn't that serious, even though she knew it was.

"Well, I had some friends unexpectedly come to town, and I hung out with them while they vacationed here in Boston. I actually wasn't even on campus, and I didn't have any messages on my door from you."

"Don't you mean one friend, a dark-skinned dude with a limousine picking you up on the same night you blew me off for tacos?" He paused and then quickly jumped back in.

"Hey, listen I get it. Why would you want to slum it with me when you've got, I mean really got, dudes with that kind of money falling all over you? It just sucked how I missed your voice message and rode up on my girl... No, nope, sorry. I guess you were not my girl but a girl I was seeing dressed like… damn! And getting in a limo with that dude. What am I supposed to feel when on top of that you don't return my calls?"

She felt for Evan because she never meant to hurt him. She had been developing feelings for him and didn't want this to happen because he'd given her something she needed when she needed it the most.

"Listen Evan, I'm so sorry that we had a miscommunication or rather that I lied. Yeah, I lied about hanging out with my friends. I met someone that really gets me, and for that short period of time I could be me and forget my problems. I never wanted to hurt your feelings. What we had was nice, but I'm in a different place right now. I can't stand it here, and I'm trying to get home. I'm just not cut out for this. My parents are making me stay here, and I'm trying to do my best to leave. It's just a matter of time before I go back to my old life in New Jersey."

He reached across the table for her hand, and she put her hand into his.

"Andy, I can't give you what that dude can right now, but I got plans and big dreams. I won't be here forever dressed in jeans and sneakers.

I'm passionate about the law and, with my grades and the promise of internships, I'll be well on my way when I'm out of here. I will have my own firm practicing law, and I'll be able to give you what you want. The house in the suburbs with the perfect lawn, kids running around, and a freaking golden retriever if you want! Whatever it is you want to do with your life, I'll support you, Andy. If you want to leave here right now and get a job here in Boston, that's cool. I'm gonna finish here and get what I came for, and we'll do fine together."

He was sincere, and as always he had it all figured out. She was the complete picture to his dreams. He would hit the ground running with a woman by his side who in good time would turn into the perfect wife. All Andrea had to do was build a life with him and support his dreams, and he would support her with the rewards of being the wife of a lawyer with the perfect life in the suburbs.

She squeezed his hand. "I love that you're a dreamer, Evan. It's like you take me on a ride with you into the future, which I have no doubt that you will make happen. But, I just don't see me in the future you have planned. I can't look out that far for myself. I don't have that kind of time. I know you're graduating soon, and I'm rooting for your success, but my life is going in a different direction. I'm sorry, Evan."

With that, she let go of his hand, stood up, and took her tray to the trash. She went out the doors of the Murph without looking back at him. On her way to her room, she thought, *one down, one to go.* If she could just keep her mind off Easton until he got on that plane, she would be fine. She just had to make it one more day, and he would be going back to his country. Then, they would both get on with their lives with no sad goodbyes.

· 7 ·

GOODBYE

Turning the key to her room door, Andrea heard her name called from down the hall. She looked.

"LaTrice?" she yelled.

"Yeah, I'm not dressed. Come down here," LaTrice yelled back.

She walked down to her room and entered to see a dressed LaTrice. Before she could question her lie, LaTrice shoved a phone in her face.

"Who is it?" Andrea asked in a whisper, but LaTrice didn't tell her.

"Hello?"

"Drea?" Easton's voice rang out. Her eyes went big as she gave LaTrice an angry face.

"Hi, East. How are you?"

"Why haven't I been able to reach you? What's going on? It's been a few days. I thought I'd give you space after you left me in the limo, but then you didn't call me. You know I leave soon. I wanted to spend as much time with you before I had to go. Are you mad at me?"

"No, no, I just had to get back to my life. You are getting back to yours, and I need to be focused here where I belong. You can understand that I needed to pull away so I can put this college thing back together, right?"

LaTrice, seeing that the conversation was delicate and personal, left the room. Andrea sat down, feeling free now to express herself better.

"I just couldn't make sense of all this, and I don't know what you want from me. I have problems that you can't solve by being my long distance boyfriend blowing into town and buying me things. This, whatever it is, is starting to hurt me, East." She was silent for a moment.

"I was hoping that you would get on the plane, and I wouldn't have to see you walk out of my life after an amazing few weeks. I needed to pull away. You understand?"

Easton sighed before speaking again. His voice was serious, and he spoke perfect English with only a slight sign that he was from the Caribbean.

"Baby, I never wanted you to feel that way. I didn't want you to feel like you had to pull away from me because I have to go. We need to talk about this and how we are going to… "

"No, Easton, I'm not doing that. Talk about what? How you are going to keep in contact with me? You want to keep what we have by phone and only plan to see me every three months when you have business here? I don't want that kind of relationship. I have to stay here at BU and graduate with no distractions or figure out how to leave. That's where I am. My parents won't let me have any other choice. I can't go home. I'm on my own in Boston." Her voice started to crack. "I gotta make this work for now."

Her emotions got the best of her, and she began to cry as she heard herself tell Easton that her father turned his back on her because of his wife and would not allow her to go home. She express the suffering she was going through.

"I didn't know you are having difficulties, Drea. I had no idea while we laughed and joked that you had problems with your parents. I needed to know what was happening with you and to you. I don't want this. I don't want this," he kept saying in a very low tone.

She could hear his distress over her situation. "I need to see you so we can talk. I can fix this. You are MY WOMAN NOW! I can't have you crying, ever, as long as I am alive. I need to see you straight away. We need to talk."

Andrea was trying to get herself under control and couldn't believe she told him about her pain over the phone. She looked around the room for some tissue to mop up her tear-filled face. When she didn't spot any, she wiped her eyes with the sleeve of her sweater, trying not to rub too hard and make her face redder than she imagined it already was.

Easton continued even though she wasn't saying anything on the other end of the phone. "Let me take you to dinner tonight, and we will come back to the suite and talk this out." Sternly, he said, "Please. I couldn't contact you, and it worried me. I don't want to feel that way about you again. Let me fix this, please." She, trying to straighten up her voice before answering him, gave him a weak ok.

"I'll be there at 6 o'clock. That's two hours from now. Get dressed up pretty, and we'll go eat first. You hear me? I'm coming for you!"

"Yes, ok, 6 o'clock. Bye, Easton."

"Drea?"

"Yes?"

"I know you can't understand yet, but I love you. I'm not telling you what I think you want to hear or trying to be with you tonight. I'm going to work this out. Okay? I love you."

"I love you too, Easton," slipped past her lips.

"Two hours!" he said.

She slowly hung up the phone. This is the goodbye she didn't want. This would be the last time, and she'd never see him again.

With LaTrice nowhere in sight, Andrea went back to her room. Making it safely back down the hall without having to explain her tear-soaked face was a relief. She began the ritual of showering, dressing, and turning into her now named persona for Easton, Drea.

She spent exactly two hours putting herself together just the way she thought Easton wanted. She wore a tight little black dress that stopped at the top of her knees with a split up the left leg to her mid-thigh. One shoulder and her whole arm were exposed, while the other shoulder and arm were fully covered by the sleeve of the dress, with a wide bell cuff at her wrist. She decided to blow her hair bone straight with a side part, letting it fall past her shoulders. Her lips were creamed red like her toes, which were exposed in her black peep-toe shoes. She popped diamond hoops into her ears and wore a matching diamond necklace. She was ready. She grabbed a wrap to cover her bare shoulder and arm.

As usual, Easton and the driver stood outside the limo waiting. When he and Andrea were in the back of the car, he immediately grabbed her and hugged her tight. When he let go, he kissed her easy so he wouldn't smear her lipstick, holding her face in both his hands. Without saying anything, she snuggled close to him to drink in the smell of his cologne. Holding her thigh with his hand, he announced they would eat first and talk later.

"I want to enjoy the view of you. You look magnificent tonight. I want to show you off to the world!" She grabbed his arm and laid her head on his shoulder.

They arrived at a seafood restaurant that sat on the side of a beautiful lake. As they entered, they could see the water, which was dotted with small floating lights. Their candlelit table was on the edge of a large dance floor, and a band was softly playing. They didn't say much during dinner. Easton's gaze from across the table made Andrea uncomfortable, and the underlying tension about the conversation they were going to have later at the hotel made this night different.

He admired her long eyelashes, which were magnified by the candlelight dancing on her face from the center of the table. After the server took the last dinner plate, the band began to play louder to encourage people to dance. Easton got up, stood in front of her, and put his hand out. The band's male singer was singing his best version of a popular love song. She looked at Easton waiting for him to tell her what to do. He finally spoke. "Please dance with me. This is our first slow dance together." She took his hand, and he led her to the dance floor where only a few couples were dancing. He swung her out and then pulled her close. They swayed easily together to the music. She got into the rhythm of following his lead, which settled her nerves.

The singer held the microphone close to his lips and crooned,

"Who's gonna love you? I'll love you forever; just give me a chance. Don't think about it; just let me love you. Who's gonna love you, baby?"

Easton swung Andrea around, and she was enjoying their dance. She felt as if they defied gravity when he glided her across the floor. Easton was a great dancer and was not afraid to show off. She was

81

thinking that he was too good to be true. He was more than she could ever ask for. The song was almost over, but she didn't want it to end. The words of the song spoke to Andrea, and she answered its question. This was what she was looking for, to be taken care of and to be loved in every way. Her heart felt that his love for her was real. This is what she needed to feel before hearing Easton's ideas about the future of their relationship. But, her mind said that this thing she felt, her heart pounding, the romance, and the love he professed after only a few weeks wasn't real at all. Easton interrupted her thoughts by kissing her hand and pulling her close in a protective embrace on the dance floor while they swayed. She felt so secure. She confirmed with herself that she would officially agree to be his woman that night and forever. She would demand to see him at least monthly. She would take that condo and living expenses. She would stay in Boston so her father wouldn't know anything except that she left BU and was working and supporting herself. As long as she was not asking to return home, she knew her father wouldn't ask any questions about her decision. She had it worked out that eventually she would convince Easton to move to the United States. Since Rodrick was his partner, he could keep an eye on their Jamaican stores so possibly Easton could go to the island every three months instead. The clapping of the other dancers interrupted her future planning, and that beautiful moment was over.

· 8 ·

ROSES ARE RED

Easton's limo was out front to whisk them away from the restaurant. The Grand Mirage Hotel was lit up so beautifully that she imagined the lights were just for them on this special occasion, as they began their life as an official couple.

As they passed the front desk holding hands, the clerk once again greeted Easton with, "Good evening, Mr. Graham," and he tilted his head to her as he always did. Once in the elevator, he tried to pull his card key from his inner jacket pocket to swipe it in the elevator so it could recognize his floor as the penthouse, but he couldn't manage it while holding her hand. He let go for a second and reached in the pocket. When he pulled out the card key, he pulled out his wallet with it. Once Andrea saw the wallet, she knew that was the heavy object she felt when she wore his jacket over her shoulders at Von Meres that first night. The leather billfold was heavy because it was stuffed three inches thick with American bills.

"East, is that money?" He chuckled while he separated the card key from his wallet and handed her the heavy wallet.

"Why do you have so much cash?"

"What do you mean?" he said.

"This is a lot to keep on you."

"I like paying in cash."

He slid the card key in the elevator slot and pushed the button for the 20th floor. She handed him back his wallet, and he put it back into his pocket. "But you always pay with a credit card at our dinners." When the elevator stopped and the doors opened, he grabbed her hand and proceeded to his suite.

"Let's have some champagne," he suggested. "But only one glass for you!" They smiled at each other as they entered the suite.

Inside there were red roses everywhere! Roses were in vases, on counters, and on tables. Rose peddles were on the floor, on shelves, and on the furniture. The whole suite was covered in red roses. The sweet smell was heavy and thick in the air. The Dom Pérignon was

85

already chilling on the table with two crystal flutes beside it. All Andrea could do was gasp. He brought her deeper into the room where she could see the whole suite was covered in red roses for her. He got down on one knee, and she couldn't believe what was happening. He held both of her hands.

"There is nothing for us to talk about, discuss, or figure out. I know it's been only a few weeks, but something happened when I met you, Drea. And I know you felt it too. I can't go on without you. I don't want to forever miss you and wonder what if. You, Drea, are the one. I need you to balance me, my life, and what I'm trying to do. You bring love and peace to me wherever I am. I need you. I don't want to hear you cry ever again. I'll fix all your problems. You don't ever have to cry as long as I breathe. I'll make it right. Baby, will you have me?"

He brought out of nowhere a midnight black velvet box. When he opened the box, the ring inside put on a light show that deserved applause! He kissed her ring finger before slipping a 10-carat diamond engagement ring on it. Andrea so surprised and overwhelmed by her emotions she dropped to her knees with him. She stared into his eyes for as long as she could until she could speak without crying.

"Yes!" she said quietly, almost in a whisper. "It would be an honor to be yours. I never imagined having the feelings I have for you, ever in my life with anybody. I thought this kind of love was only in fairytales and TV shows, but meeting you changed everything. You're my knight in shining armor, and for me the fairytale came true. I love you, Easton!"

Kneeling there together, they kissed. They were not rushed or out of control. They kissed with the assurance that they had all night and a whole lifetime ahead of them to make love. It felt right and in every way it was.

· 9 ·

THE TRUTH

The next morning, they lay in Easton's bed together. Andrea tried to remember every moment of their lovemaking, from the moment it started in the living room until they moved into to the bedroom. She had never had sex with the power of love behind it. Easton was a man, a real man who showed her his love with his gentle touch and strong passion. All she could think about now was getting married to a wealthy man she loved and who loved her too. She knew their love was unstoppable.

Andrea stayed at The Grand Mirage with Easton all that day and a second night. He changed his flight, which was scheduled to leave the next day. The thought of him getting on that plane now was even more painful, but she would handle it better knowing that she was now on a mission to find an apartment until he came back to buy her a condominium. She would be busy setting up her new place and leaving school to start her new life. She needed to iron out the details and timelines of when exactly they would be living under one roof and when their wedding would be. When the thoughts were too overwhelming to sort out, she just looked at her engagement ring, and it all floated away. Easton also had a timeline that concerned him. He wondered when he would tell her that she had to pack and join him on the trip back to Jamaica. He had one more day before it was time to go.

That night, they decided to finish watching LaTrice's movie. They stretched out on the couch together, with her in between his legs and practically on top of him lying backwards. Andrea held the popcorn bowl on her stomach while eating and passed kernels into Easton's mouth over her shoulder. The Boston skyline twinkled in the background through the clear floor-to-ceiling windows. Again, they started talking during the movie and didn't really pay attention.

"Listen, my plane leaves tomorrow. You need to be on it with me, Drea." She turned around and sat upright so she could see his face. Her ponytail bounced around with her quick movement.

"What do you mean? Aren't you coming back to look for a home for us? I figured you would go home to check on your business and come back. Your home base would now be here in Boston, and you could go to Jamaica every few months to check in, but you would live here with me. Isn't that the plan?"

Easton now sat up too, and with a distracted look gently pulled one of her springy curls from her ponytail and watched it bounce back when it slipped through his fingers.

"Drea, I can't live here."

"Why not?"

"My business won't allow it. My business is in Jamaica. I only come here to deal with people who live here, and after a while I won't need to come here at all."

"What are you talking about, Easton? Rodrick is your partner. Can't he take care of the stores in Jamaica while you take care of the people you need to deal with here?"

Looking straight into her face, Easton said, "Drea, I can't live here because I'm not here legally. There are no stores in Jamaica. Rodrick is not my partner; he works for me. We are not here to buy merchandise for stores." He hesitated for a second. "I'm here on drug business."

There was a long pause with the two staring at each other. Before that could soak into her brain, he continued talking. "I don't deal in merchandise… I deal in drugs. I need you to hear me. I never meant to deceive you baby. Our meeting was an accident. There was no way for me to tell you the truth until we got to this point."

Andrea was shocked and stunned by what she heard. She just sat and stared at him with a blank look as he continued.

"I'm not a bad guy, Drea. It's just my business. I'm practically invisible. I'm not slinging dope on street corners. I make things happen much higher. The man I report to is like a father to me, and I'm well protected. I've been in and out of the U.S. for years, since I was a teenager, handling business with people here. I don't carry drugs, I just make the deals. I want you to know that I meant everything I said, and I can give you everything you want, but just not here in the Unites States. Baby, you have to get on the plane and come home with me."

Andrea tried to snap out of the shock of hearing her fiancé tell her that he is some kind of drug dealer from Jamaica and there are no stores and he's not in the U.S. to buy wholesale merchandise for those stores, but to make drug deals.

"I don't know what you're saying to me right now!" she shouted. "Are you telling me that this whole thing is a lie? That you are not who I think you are? That when you proposed to me, the life I have planned is not the life I can have with you? You want me to leave my country and become the wife of a criminal? Is that what you are saying to me?"

She began to get hysterical and jumped up from the couch. "I am so dumb!" she shouting to the ceiling.

Easton hadn't expected her to lose it the way she did. He didn't know what to do. He didn't deal well with situations that he couldn't control. He kept trying to interject in her shouting with reasonable solutions and explanations, but it wasn't working.

"Drea, are you going to let this get in the way of the life we can have?"

"Easton! You are a drug dealer!" she shouted at him. "I can't live a life of illegal activity that could land you or me in jail. What are you asking me to do?" she cried. "What kind of life are you asking me to live?"

She put both her hands over her face and sobbed uncontrollably. He stood up from the couch with his heart beating fast and walked over to her and removed her hands from her face. He bent down to look at her.

"Sit down next to me and let me tell you what really is the truth," he said. "Please, I need you to calm down."

She allowed him to lead her back to the couch and they sat side by side.

"First, the highest risk for me is here in the U.S. which is why I can't live here. In Jamaica, I rule," he said while beating his chest with one of his fists. "I'm protected there, and so will you be. The DEA can't do nothing with me in Jamaica. When I come here, it's trickier, but to be safe it's well orchestrated. When I arrive, I'm clean, and when I leave here, I'm still clean. People all along the way are greased, I mean paid, to make sure I have no problems here and that I stay safe. Drea, I'm the boss of this operation."

She listened with her head down, tears dropping while she rolled her new diamond around on her slim finger.

"There are people here to look after me that you and nobody else ever see."

She looks up at him, "Rodrick?"

"No, Rodrick works for me, but he has a job that is not about my protection."

"What about LaTrice?" she asked.

"What about her?"

"She knows about all this and was a part of tricking me?"

Shaking his head, "I don't know why LaTrice brought you to me that night. We thought she would have replaced the girl who didn't show with someone who knew the deal and would be paid at the end of my trip. I quickly realized that you didn't know, and I liked you. You were with me and kept being with me because you wanted to, because of me. You wanted nothing from me. Do you know that a man in my position doesn't know anyone, I mean no one, who doesn't want something. That was okay with me until I met you."

He stood up and walked over to the wall made of glass and looked out over the city with his back to her. "You did something to me, girl. You turned me inside out. I didn't know what else to do but make you mine. I had no part in selecting you that night. LaTrice should have known better. That's what she gets paid for."

"I still don't get how she fits into all of this," she said.

Andrea's mind was spinning as she tried to understand how and why her new world just came crashing down. She wiped her eyes with a napkin that was on the coffee table for the popcorn.

"LaTrice is just some girl we hired to give us a reason to be here. She is not really Rodrick's girlfriend. She is getting paid with things and cash money. How it works is they pretend to be together, and he plays the part all the way by doing what she asks and paying for what she needs for the time he's here. She likes him enough. He gets the perks of being her boyfriend a few times a year, but the bottom line is she's a part of my association hired to make sure women are available for my men and for me as well when we come to town. Never should she have gotten a woman who didn't know the game. But that's all small stuff. I don't get involved with matching people up for appearances. I'm next to the boss, and my job is bigger than that mess. She really messed up, Andrea, and I'm sorry we're here now trying to figure this out. But I'm so glad you landed in my life. I love you, and we're gonna make this work."

Andrea's face still showed concern, and Easton knew he wasn't making her any more comfortable by explaining things, but he needed to tell her the truth. She knew enough to know he was a kingpin in the drug world.

Easton walked back to the couch where Andrea was sitting. "My home is Jamaica. There I live the life I want. You have to trust me right here, right now. I have to go home, Drea, people are waiting for me. I have to do my job."

Andrea kissed his face in several places, wetting his dark smooth skin with her tears. Then she went to his bedroom. When she came out and walked by him, she had all her things and kept walking right out the door.

· 10 ·

DORM LOVE

Andrea's dorm room was a drastic change from the penthouse at The Grand Mirage. After dropping her things down on the bed, she headed right to LaTrice's room, but there was no answer when she knocked. She returned to her room, looked around, and declared out loud to the furniture, "Well, I'm back. That's it. I have to be happy here until I figure out how to get out of this hellhole and still have shoes on my feet." The furniture listened without judgment, but she was judging herself harshly. Before she could gather her thoughts and begin to plan how to make up homework and excuses for missing classes again, she needed sleep. The stress had worn her out, and all she could do now was sleep.

She slept all that night and half of the next day. Her stomach was growling for food, but she ignored it because the pain in her heart was much greater. She decided she would start reaching out to professors and teachers and explain her absence from classes by giving them a sob story about being ill or about a family member who passed away. But contacting them would have to wait because she couldn't get out of bed that day either. It was the day Easton was on the plane heading back to his life in Jamaica. She told herself she would bounce back from this, but she couldn't do it. The pain was getting deeper.

That evening, she made herself soup in the microwave, took a shower, changed her sheets, and straightened up her room. She was trying to get it together for the next day's tasks of getting back on track with her classes.

The door thumped with a heavy knock. She looked at it with anger. She thought for sure this was the girl she wanted to see! Snatching the door open ready to accuse and question LaTrice, her angry face changed in a split second to a pout and furrowed eyebrows when her eyes fell on Easton. She jumped into his arms, buried her head in his neck, and wrapped her legs around his waist as she sobbed. He carried her fully into the room, closing the door behind him without letting go of her. He gently sat on the bed and continued to hold her while she cried. He rubbed her back and let her tears flow, not saying anything. Andrea eventually took her face out of his tear drenched neck and looked up at him, sad and confused.

He softly said, "I'm gonna fix this too. I'm gonna do what it takes." Not knowing what that meant and not having the energy to hear or comprehend much of anything, she didn't ask. She just wanted to enjoy him while he was still there, in her space, right now. She continued to sit on his lap, softly talking about what she had been doing the last few days. Soon, her sadness faded away and she felt more like her old self. She even smiled. He kissed her, and she grabbed him around his neck and kissed him back.

Unlike the lovemaking at The Grand Mirage after his proposal, there was now a new energy, fueled by the possibility of not being able to see each other again. Andrea snatched off him whatever clothes she could while trying to throw him backwards on the bed. She wanted to release all her anger to the sex they were about to have. He matched her angry passion and gripped her with equal force without hurting her, but rough enough to show her that he was the man. He held her wrists together over her head with one hand. Together they rolled violently a few times, each struggling to be the aggressor. Easton could clearly overpower her but let her think she had the upper hand at times. He loved her assertiveness and let her get a few moves in before taking it back and squeezing her tighter than he would normally to give her what she wanted, a fight without actually throwing punches. She was angry at him but wanted to love him at the same time. He was sweating, trying to control her. They'd give each other pleasure for a moment and then go back to wrestling over the next position.

When the fight in her was gone and her anger lifted, they finally hit a euphoric zone she had never known before. Their lovemaking was in perfect sync. For Andrea, everything in the room blacked out around her except for Easton. It was like she had tunnel vision with just him in sight. She couldn't hear any sound or catch her breath. A beam of heat shot through her body. She wanted nothing else but this drug, his presence, his body, his love. He was feeling the same and knew he was hooked for life. He was squeezing her wrists harder and harder without realizing it. They both made sounds they'd never made before as they reached a place they'd never been before.

Collapsed side by side in silence, Easton pulled Andrea closer to his sweaty body and whispered in her ear, "Are you hurt?"

She whispered back. "No. I love you."

Completely rung out, they slept.

Over the next couple of days, they stayed in the dorm together. They watched TV, ordering Chinese, pizza, and burgers for their meals. They read parts of books to each other out loud not finishing even one of them. Cuddled up in bed reading was not about finishing the books or understanding the stories but about the experience they were having together. Andrea was in shorts and a T-shirt, and Easton was wearing boxers and his undershirt since the room was always too warm because she couldn't control the heat in the dorm. A cracked window and less clothes worked for them both.

Easton stood next to her shelves in the room looking at the pictures of her on top of the pyramid of the cheerleading squad.

"So you were really a cheering girl?" he laughed.

"Yeah look, that's me up there." She said.

"Wow, Drea, that's something!" He moved from the wall photos to flipping through photo albums with pictures of her and her friends posing for the camera at various places like the Jersey Shore, the local pizza shop, the mall, and poolside at Andrea's house. Her prom pictures were there too, and he wanted to know about her date.

"That's my ex-boyfriend," she pointed out.

"How did he let you get away?" he asked without removing his eyes from the picture.

"He didn't let me do anything. We agreed we would break up when we graduated. We didn't love each other." she said nonchalantly.

"How come he didn't love you?"

"I don't know. We just fit, and our parents liked the idea. So we dated."

"Were you ever in love, Drea?"

She hated to confess that she hadn't been, ever.

"Nope, Easton, I haven't. Not until I met you."

That made her extra special in his eyes…that he was the first man to capture her heart. He turned the page of the album and saw a picture of the quarterback in his uniform posing with Drea in her cheerleader warm-up suit. Her hair was in a ponytail tied with a big red ribbon. He couldn't believe he got the cheerleader from the suburbs by day and a knockout by night. Looking at her hugging the quarterback made him kind of jealous, so he closed the album and turned his attention to her.

"Hey, bouncy gal, can ya give me a cheer right here, right now?"

Andrea laughed and laid on the bed next to where he was sitting.

102

"What? You want me to do a cheer for you?"

"Yah mon, show me what yu got."

She grabbed the pom-poms from the shelf over her bed and got ready to oblige his request, wearing her cut-off sweatpants and a half-shirt that read "Scotch Plains Football XXL". Easton spread himself across the queen-sized bed lying on his side, propped up on one elbow with a big grin on his face to watch her cheer for him.

"Ready team, OK!" she shouted before a series of high kicks and arm moves with her pom-poms. She began to chant her cheer.

Easton Graham, he's our man. If he can't do it, nobody can!

Go Easton! Fight Graham! Let's go! Easton Graham!

"Woooo!!!" she yelled while moving the pom-poms in a rolling motion over her head. He clapped with the biggest grim on his face as she dropped the pom-poms on the floor and dove back onto the bed next to him.

"Wow, you made that up just for me?"

"No, it's the cheer we did for the quarterback. I just inserted your name."

"Ahhh, I see. Then it was that other dude's cheer! Well then, it was kinda corny!"

As he laughed, she grabbed a pillow and bopped him over the head with it.

"No, really, I love that about you. You didn't even know it was corny," he said while continuing to laugh.

"But, Drea, the fact that you did it because I asked you to is what makes me love you."

She planted a kiss on him and rolled off the bed to find a menu to figure out what they were going to eat for dinner. They were running out of take-out places.

For dinner that night, Andrea went to the Murph and picked up sandwiches, potato chips, and chocolate milk. She brought it back to the room where she was hiding her lover.

They both knew this couldn't last much longer but didn't want to talk about it yet. They just wanted to shut the outside world out while they enjoyed each other in simple ways.

Over the dry sandwiches, Andrea asked Easton about Jamaica and where he came from. He told her that he grew up in the Grans, West Kingston.

"It was hard there. The streets is all there is. You gotta survive or you die."

"Are your parents still there?"

"Well, my mom died, Drea, when I was a young boy. She got cancer, and because we were poor, she had no medical care so she died quickly. I was raised by a lady who lived next door to us, Auntie. She wasn't my aunt, but she took me in. It was rough trying to make it where murder, drugs, and guns were everywhere. My goal was to survive by being a part of the crime scene without getting killed myself. I just tried to grow up fast, so I could get my Auntie out of there and set up in a house where she didn't have to work cleaning hotels and taking the buses back and forth to feed me. Even as a boy, I ran drugs for money. I had to. There were no other options for me."

He took another bite of his sandwich and continued to tell of his youth in Kingston.

"My Auntie is gone now. She died five years ago, but she saw my success. I had her living in a big house finally resting. I would go see her, give her money, and let her feed me." He smiled remembering her. "I'm thankful I was able to do that for her. She didn't have to take me in when my mom died. She couldn't afford me, but she did what she could, always. She enjoyed what I could give her. Now I live in Hunter's Bay in Saint Lawrence Parish where the beach is my back yard. I'm under a very powerful man in Jamaica. I command a crew that brings money to my boss above all the others who are trying to make underboss. But that doesn't matter really, that I bring the most money, because he picked me. He has no sons, and I had no father, brothers, or uncles. He taught me from a boy. I'm next in line."

He stopped his talk about his organization and tried to bring the conversation back to his upbringing. "Well, anyway, I had no one else except her, my Auntie. I had no relatives. I never knew my father. I grew up alone just me and my Auntie. She was the only one who loved me. I desperately wanted a family, a real family. Now it's my time to be corny, right?" He smiled a painful smile.

"No, that's not corny. Everyone wants and deserves to be loved by family, East. You mean you never loved anyone else either, no girlfriend?"

A bright smile now appeared while he looked down into his sandwich. His head tilted to the side. *"Yah I get di girls and tings you know, di in and out ting,"* he joked.

Andrea felt a twinge of jealousy imagining another woman having sex with her Easton, but she didn't let it show.

"Nothing serious then?"

"No, not serious. One friend back home who was business, but more like something to do. No real affection for her."

She figured he was saying that the semi-girlfriend started out as business, which landed them in bed a few times. She wasn't worried. She was the one wearing his ring she told herself.

The next night, as they lay looking up at the ceiling in deep thought, Andrea noticed how much facial hair Easton had now. She rubbed it lovingly, while he made a face as if it hurt. "Itchy," he complained.

She jumped on him and straddled him, looking into his face. "It's nice. I like it! It's sexy. I've never seen you scruffy. You're always perfect, right down to your designer underwear!"

He reached up and rubbed his waved-up hair back and forth, squinting while saying, "I need a haircut too. See what I've become for you?"

They laughed, and he snatched her into a bear hug, threw her down on the other side of the bed, and rolled on top of her growling and gritting his teeth playfully like a bear attacking her. Wrapping herself completely around him and squeezing back, their tussle heated up the love flame once more.

Andrea snuck Easton into the showers late at night, after everyone was in bed and there was practically no chance of seeing anyone. Being very quiet, they showered together and enjoyed the simulation of a life together. With still no talk of how long he would be with her, she enjoyed every moment.

By the fifth day, she started getting notices by mail and phone messages stuck to the outside of her door from the university asking where she was.   And after that, she received a notice of dismissal from the school. Since she hadn't responded to a request to report to the dean of student's office, it was bound to happen. Once the final notice came officially dismissing her, Easton made his move.

Gently he told her, "It's time for me to go now." She ignored his statement. "I need you to come with me. You can come back to the States when I come, if that makes it easier for you."

She still didn't respond. "What do you have here anymore, Drea?"

"I need to think and work this out," she finally said.

"I thought that's what you were doing all this time we spent in this room, seeing what it would be like just me and you," he said.

With a deep release of breath, she said, "I need more time. I need to leave here, pack up, go home, and settle things there with my

108

parents. I somehow thought that, when you asked me to marry you, we would live here. I can't leave the country. And I'm still trying to deal with the fact you're a drug dealer!"

Andrea shook her head in disbelief that she was weighing two difficult options; either show up at home hoping they let her in, or leave the country with a criminal.

"Easton, I don't do drugs. I don't know about drugs or illegal activities. I wasn't raised that way. Who would I be to accept that life? I love you, but this changes everything. You are asking me to go against…. I don't know what, but it's bad," she said calmly.

"I don't have any more time, Drea. I'm way past my time here. I've missed meetings, check-ins, and appointments. What I don't need is people looking for me because I haven't fulfilled my obligations here. I'll arrange your ticket to travel with me tomorrow morning. I'll be waiting for you to arrive back at the hotel by 6 am, ready to take this step with me."

He reached over and held her hands in his. "I don't want trouble with your parents. You should speak with them. I wish I could stay longer and visit your home with you to make them properly comfortable, but there just isn't time. I love you and want you. I hope you want me as much."

He let go of her hands and made his way to the door. Before opening it to leave, he said, "I hope you choose me."

With that, he left her there, doubting in his own mind that he would be able to board that plane without her.

· 11 ·

TIME TO GO

Packing up her room was a more depressing task than she expected it would be. This is what she wanted from the first week at BU, but going home this way wouldn't be easy. She booked her flight to New Jersey for the next day with the credit card from her father. She planned to ship her boxes to arrive after she did. The room was empty and lonely without Easton. But she couldn't dwell on it because she had to be out before they came around to physically throw her out.

Suddenly, LaTrice busted into the room like she was being chased by the Boogie Man. The unlocked door swung open and scared Andrea. LaTrice was uncharacteristically scattered and rushed, and that frightened Andrea. LaTrice quickly got to it.

"Look, Easton sent me!"

"What? He was just here this morning. He knows how to reach me. Why would he send you," Andrea sarcastically shot at her. "You of all people, who can't be trusted!"

"Ok fine, doesn't matter who sent me. You need to move from here now. I came to get you and to explain life to your princess ass. You are getting on the plane! You have no choice. Easton forgot who he is, messing with you! He missed another call this morning layin' up here. I don't know what kinda tricks you put on him to have him all open to where he is messin' up his game, his money, and MY money!"

"My?" Andrea questioned.

"Listen, my money is wrapped up in this business too. A lot of people are on the line here with this trip, and you are messin it up. You have no idea, girl, what you are into here and how this is affecting powerful people. More powerful people than Easton! Hey, I never meant to put you in this position, but the girl I had lined up to occupy Easton didn't come through at the last minute. I needed him to be with someone while he was here, so it looked right, that's all. To my surprise, he started falling for you. Well, that didn't seem to be such a problem cause I thought you would follow the money trail and get all you could get out of him like I do with Rod. It's all part of the job.

The job gets you money, shopping, outings with limos, and sex if you want it. The more legit it looks, the better. You could have had him setting you up, coming here every few months and spending that cash on you. And when you graduated, you could walk away if you wanted. Your time here would have been more than comfortable. That's what you needed, right? But no, you wanted more. You wanted it all and played that love game. Cool, it worked! He's all boxed up with you and offering you the world. So what's the damn problem, girl?" she shouted.

Andrea couldn't get a word in edgewise, so she let LaTrice go on since she was so upset.

"I know you and your type, whining all the time cause your suburban life wasn't enough. Man after man trying to get more and more. I'm not knocking your hustle, but that is beyond lazy; it's a sickness. Take my word, this is the top of what you are ever going to be offered, so if I were you, I'd take it. Get on the plane and let him take care of you. I need you to get on the plane so he gets on the plane. You understand?"

"I don't know what you're talking about, LaTrice. I'm packing to go home, and Easton knows that."

She turns her back to LaTrice and placed one last item in an open box.

"What is really happening, Andrea, is that you have gotten in the way of some very dangerous people who will harm you to get Easton back on track. If he had gone home, we wouldn't be having this conversation. But now you, the distraction, could be eliminated unless you get on the plane or better yet, disappear so he has no choice but to go home without you. Easton was given the same message, that if he doesn't get about the business, his distraction will be taken care of. So it's up to you. Disappear if you just can't compromise your morals and be with him."

Convinced she had given Andrea enough to think about, LaTrice left.

What Andrea didn't know, but Easton did know, was that the threat against her, didn't come from Easton's boss but from leaders under the same boss; their money was also wrapped up in the Boston deal. They got nervous when Easton came up shaky. They started to tail him when he changed his flight and Rodrick returned home without him. Easton sent Rodrick back with a message that he had everything under control. He also sent the security people, who always went wherever he went, back as well. It was unheard of for him to be without security, especially in a foreign country. That's what tipped them off that something was wrong. He had gone against every protocol.

A scheme was set in motion to get him back to Jamaica before the talk of his actions stirred the big boss which could pull the plug on all the money they were about to make. The men behind the scheme would defiantly resort to eliminating Andrea as they promised by phone to Easton if he held up any longer.

Andrea stopped packing and sat down on the bed to think. She couldn't believe this was happening. She didn't know how to process what LaTrice had told her. She thought about sticking to the plan of going home. If Easton showed up in New Jersey, she knew her father would have no problem telling him she wasn't there. Then he would have no choice but go back to Jamaica.

An unknown voice with thoughts very different from her own told her she was a strong woman and could get a job, that she didn't need a successful man to take care of her. She could get an apartment, work in the city, and buy her own designer purses.

In slow motion, she took the deepest breath of her life and threw her head back to fill her lungs to capacity. On the slow release, she shut all the thoughts down in her head and went to the hall to make a call.

"Yello," the voice rang out over the line.

"Hi, Dad, it's me."

"Hey there, what's going on, baby? You need money?"

"No, Dad."

She spoke in her little girl voice that always worked on her father when she was trying to make him feel guilty.

"I just wanted to let you know that I'm leaving school and…

"Oh no, you promised you would try. I just can't believe you didn't give it a chance!"

He couldn't hide the disappointment in his voice, he went on and on until there was nothing else to say.

"Well, I'll get you a ticket, and you can move back in your room until we figure out what to do next."

"Dad, I'm not staying at school, but I'm not coming home either."

"What do you mean, Andy?"

Struggling to keep it together, she told an elaborate lie about going to Jamaica with a group of friends she made in Boston who were from the island. She explained that there were lots of opportunities at the resorts for Americans who could learn the service industry in a place where tourism was so high. She said she would come home with skills to get a hotel management job anywhere in the U.S. She rattled on about her exotic travel plans to Jamaica.

He seemed impressed with the details of her plans and praised her ability to switch gears so quickly when college life wasn't working out. He was relieved that he wouldn't have to tell Lorraine that she would be coming back home.

"That sounds good, sweetheart. When will you leave?"

"Sometime next week, Dad."

"Well, you call me when you arrive and let us know where you will be staying. I'll send you a little extra something to get you started over there. You still have the credit card, right?"

"Yes, I still have it." Trying not to break up, she steadied her voice.

"I'll call you in a few weeks.   I'll make you proud, Dad."

"Well, ok then, baby. I love you!"

"Love you too, Dad."

She went to her hidden safe behind the wall and took her jewelry out and placed it in her carry-on bag. She had all her boxes packed up and ready to ship to Scotch Plains. She knew her Dad would accept them and wouldn't think it odd when they showed up. Only her most expensive clothes and a few pairs of shoes made it into the one bag she was taking. Her load felt finally light.

· 12 ·

BLUER SKIES

The limo ride to the airport was long and quiet. Instead of Boston's Logan International Airport, they were heading to Bradley International Airport in Connecticut. Easton was unusually preoccupied with his own thoughts. He was oddly not in tune with her. As if he were an athlete, he had his game face on. He was in boss mode and back on his game. Andrea wanted to know why they were driving all the way to Connecticut.

Quickly Easton told her in a scolding manner, "From here on, I need our movements to be flawless. I need you to trust me and do what I say; the less words the better. I have everything under control. Do what I say, Drea, and we will get home safe and surrounded by my people. Careful and steady we have to be while we travel. Ok?"

119

Andrea nodded and stopped talking. They each had just one carry-on bag, which were on the seat next to Andrea. She noticed several colorful brochures sticking up from the outside pocket of Easton's bag. She pulled them out and laid them on her lap. Easton didn't stop her. They were brochures for Jamaica. One was about the history, another showed the best resorts, and the last was a map of the whole island showing the parishes, towns, beaches, and airports. She read all of them front to back since they would be in the limo for a while.

Andrea found out that Kingston was the capitol and a very busy city with lots of business energy. Most tourists visited the coastal areas where the palatial resorts sat with all the amenities vacationers could want and need. The average temperature was around 85 degrees with sunny skies. One brochure informed her that Jamaica gained full independence from the United Kingdom in 1962. Its motto was: "Out of many, one people." She also learned that Jamaica's population is made-up of many ethnicities, which were African, East Indian, Chinese, and European, which made them one people, Jamaicans. The Jamaican flag waved with a yellow X that divided the colors green and black. Two major airports, located on opposite ends of the island, carried local and international passengers. Norman Manley

International Airport was in Kingston, and Sangster International Airport was in Montego Bay. She wondered why they were flying into Montego Bay after looking up where St. Lawrence Parish was in the brochure. Norman Manley International was right in Kingston next to St. Lawrence. She didn't dare ask Easton because he was still tense, with his jaw clenched, looking out the window. Andrea thought all the facts about her new home were interesting, and the photos were beautiful.

When she finished reading, she refolded the brochures and stuck them back in the side pocket of Easton's bag, shoving them down deep so they wouldn't be lost. Easton immediately reached in the side pocket and pulled them back up, so that they were sticking out the way she found them.

As they approached the check-in counter at Bradley International Airport, Andrea had no idea what was next. Easton produced tickets, U.S. passports, and two Boston driver licenses. After he flashed his pearly white teeth, the woman at the counter dressed in a vibrant multicolored jumper, smiled at him flirtatiously.

"Vacation?" she asked with a smirk after noticing Andrea by his side.

"Honeymoon," he responded patting his carry-on right on top of the brochures sticking up from the side pocket. He then looked lovingly at his bride.

"Oh, that's nice," the agent said, disappointed.

She handed back his documents, saying, "Congratulations Mr. Williams and Mrs. Williams. Enjoy your honeymoon. You are at gate 88A. You can proceed to your left."

Before the agent could finish her instructions, Easton grabbed Andrea's hand and headed to their gate. They sat in silence at gate 88A watching people gather. Vacationers, honeymooners, and native Jamaicans making their way home were among the growing crowd. Easton leaned over to her and asked, "You hungry?"

"A little. All the food counters and kiosks smell really good," she said.

"Let's go get something," he responded while standing up. "We're on our honeymoon, so let's act like it," he joked and then planted a loving kiss on her lips. For the first time that morning, he was her East again.

They made their way through the airport to a bar at a T.G.I. Friday's that was within earshot of boarding announcements. They had a little time to kill before they expected to hear an announcement for their flight to Montego Bay.

Easton had a cold beer and ordered her a coke and cheeseburger. When her order arrived, he looked her in the eyes and said, "I'm putting something in your drink."

"What?"

"I need you to be smooth and calm. Everything will go fine, but I can't get us into Jamaica the way I need to if I'm worried about you. I need you to be cool. I'm not knocking you out, Drea. It's just a sedative that will make you sleep on the flight and keep you calm when we have to navigate the airport in Mo 'Bay. You trust me?"

She just looked him directly in the eyes for a moment. He didn't blink.

"Yes, I trust you." He dropped a few pink pills in her coke.

"Eat first, baby," he said.

Andrea ate and downed her coke after the pills were well dissolved. He made small talk that didn't make any sense to her when someone came near them. She played along because she realized he was nervous and didn't trust anyone.

When they were finished, they held hands on the way back to gate 88A. She noticed he held her closer than before. He whispered that he had her and would not let her fall if she felt the sedative working. She held him closer too, not knowing what to expect from the pink pills.

Getting to their first-class seats was a relief for her because she was now feeling it. Finally settling down in her window seat was like making it to home plate. The in-flight announcements, the takeoff, and the flight attendants moving back in forth were all a blur. She was soon out cold, wrapped in an aircraft blanket and leaning against her protector, the man who would give her everything, the man she was trusting with everything.

Over four hours later, Easton was gently trying to rouse her by calling her name softly and rubbing her cheek. She opened one eye at a time and for a second didn't remember where she was or what was going on. It took a minute for it all to come back to her.

He whispered, "We are about to land. Look out the window. That's my home, our home."

They were approaching an oddly shaped island with the most beautiful crystal blue water surrounding it. She could see coconut palm trees swaying in the wind and had no doubt it was a warm wind. The

124

sun sparkled off the blue water. Andrea saw every shade of blue, from the deepest part of the ocean to the shallow waters lapping onto the beaches. The sky was also blue, a pale welcoming blue with big fluffy white clouds floating under it. She wanted to land and enjoy all of Jamaica's tropical blues.

Suddenly, the plane's engine started to cut back in power, and Andrea could feel the plane's descent throughout her entire body. She looked at Easton in fear and said, "I'm gonna be sick. I'm coming out of this sedative, and I'm gonna throw up!"

"Let's go," he said.

They both jumped up and headed to the plane's front bathroom. Before the flight attended could protest, they were both jammed in the tiny closet of a bathroom with the door locked. She let loose what she had eaten over the tiny metal toilet. She could tell it was just nausea caused by the pills Easton gave her. She had flown often for vacations with her father and Lorraine and was never sick. She stood up shaking, with no room to move, squeezed up against Easton who looked concerned. She laid her head on his chest for a minute and enjoyed the cool forced air coming from the ceiling. It was the air that supplied circulation for the bathroom. It hit her right in the face, cooling her sweat and her nerves at the same time. They stood against each other in silence with his arms wrapped around her as if it was halftime and, no matter what, they needed to go back out and finish the game.

He pulled away as much as he could so she could turn around to the tiny sink and splash water on her face.

"You ok?" he asked while she pat her face dry with a hard brown paper towel.

"I'm good, just really sleepy still and stiff. East? Is someone gonna hurt me?"

"No! I wouldn't bring you to Jamaica if that were the case. I just need to get home so I can meet with some people and reassure them that I have everything under control. I needed to show my face in Jamaica before they found me in Boston. I'm back now, so there's no need for anyone to come looking for me. Now that I have you with me and I'm handling everything, it will all work out. You have nothing to be afraid of. You will be my wife now! Respect!" he said harshly. "Everyone must respect *dat*. We gotta just get through Customs on this side, and we're fine."

Back in their first-class seats and properly buckled up, Andrea and Easton where almost there. The water was even bluer and more spectacular as they got closer to it!

· 13 ·

HIS JAMAICA

"*Welcome* to Sangster International Airport in Montego Bay, Jamaica,"

rang out over the intercom throughout the aircraft. "The temperature

is a beautiful 87 degrees with clear skies. If you are here on vacation,

we hope that you enjoy your stay with us, and if you are *Jah-May-Con*,

welcome home!"

With her carry-on in hand and sunglasses on, Andrea walked arm

in arm with Easton down the stairs connected to the aircraft. She

teetered a bit, not at the steepness but because the sedative was still

slowing her down. The portable stairs led right onto the tarmac. The

sun was blazing and baking the heads of passengers from the East

Coast of the U.S., who were not used to it. The Jamaican air was hot,

dry, and dusty. The airport entrance was a short walk across the tarmac.

Once inside the airport, Andrea noticed there was no air-conditioning! Large fans hanging from the ceiling just spread hot air around hot people.

She wanted to panic, thinking the brochures lied to her and now she was in what looked like a Third World country that she had to call home, but the sedative wouldn't let her react.

Easton moved through Sangster without a word or a facial expression. He let go of his steadying hold and walked next to her. They came to a line at a group of tables that looked like picnic tables. People were putting their carry-on bags and belongings on the tables for airport personnel to check. Bags were being unzipped as gloved hands gently searched inside. Once cleared, the bags were re-zipped and handed back to the owner so they could proceed to Customs.

Andrea and Easton stood in line and waited their turn. Both bags were searched, put back together, and handed back to them. She followed Easton staying close by his side. Right before they reached a wall of rowed-off closed doors leading into the main airport, he handed her a blue American passport with a loose piece of paper stuck inside the pages.

"Here is your passport. I'm going to separate from you and go to a different line in the customs area. Show them your passport, and I'll meet you on the other side. Don't worry. I won't be far away, it will go smooth."

She opened the passport, knowing it wasn't hers, just to see the name inside. It read Tamara Williams, born in Greenville, Mississippi, with a picture of a woman who looked similar to her. They walked through the rowed-off doors to a rush of people passing by. She looked all around and saw souvenirs stacked up the walls of shops for sale to the departing tourist, then she smelled the food that was also for sale. It was very different form the T.G.I. Friday's she had lunch at in the American airport.

Everyone in the airport was dressed for vacation, while the airport workers all seemed overdressed for the kind of heat that vibrated across the island and even inside the airport. She noticed that the only people sweating were the tourists. The airport personnel were professionally dressed alike. All white shirts were crisp and tucked in without a wrinkle in site. Their black shoes glossed to reflection. The men were well groomed, and the women looked like the black beauties on the popular Fashion Fair Cosmetics posters at the malls back in the U.S.

Andrea tried to take in the dated décor, antiquated shops, and the 70s light green Customs booths they were approaching. This was no London Heathrow, Chicago O'Hare, or even Newark International Airport in New Jersey for that matter. There were more things to look at than her slow mind could see. She was intrigued that there were so many black people in every capacity running the airport from the pilots, to security, to the Customs officers and even the shopkeepers. It was like nothing she'd ever seen before, and it made her smile. Her travels with her parents internationally had always been to European countries.

She and Easton headed towards the Customs lines. Like he said, he went to the furthest left line, and she stayed in the middle line.

A mysterious security guard appeared and seemed to be hovering near her. She tried not to look at him and convinced herself that he was just monitoring the lines the same way they did in the U.S., the U.K., and in other countries' Custom's areas. She wondered about Easton's passport while she stood waiting. What was the fictitious name on his? Andrea liked the name Tamara and wondered if that's what she would be called from then on. She watched Easton across the way. He was almost at the counter. She didn't see him holding the blue passport he presented in the U.S. but a different one. She squinted and could see the passport he was now holding was a red-ish color. She saw him reach the counter and present his passport without any words to the agent. The agent handed it back and sent Easton through to the other side. The hovering security guard now seemed to be walking in circles, but his circle walking moved down the line as she moved closer to the counter so his movements never stopped.

Finally, it was her turn. She smiled and handed the male agent her passport with the paper inside. In a Jamaican accent, the agent called her name, *"TAM-MA-RAH WILL-YUMS?"*

"Yes, Tamara Williams, that's me."

"Travelin' alone?"

"Yes sir. I'm meeting friends here for vacation."

Now pointing to the loose paper stuck inside of the passport, he asked, "Where are you staying? You didn't list it here on the Declaration Form."

She froze for a second trying to think of the right answer. She remembered the brochure and tried to pull a resort that she read about from her head, but the drug was still affecting her. Calmly she responded, "I'm sorry, umm, I'm going to Runaway Bay. I'm staying at Sandals."

Without looking at her again, the agent stamped her passport and handed it back to her while his eyes moved to the next person in line.

When she was on the other side, she searched for Easton. She saw him leaning against the wall near a shop that had wall-to-wall bottles of liquor with black, yellow, and green flags everywhere.

As she was about to reach him, a woman eased up to her saying, *"Hello, sista. Ya want great fun while ya here in Jah-May-Ca? Mi got cheap Dunn's River passes. Discount passes to di falls. Come wit' mi dis way."*

Before Andrea could muster up a response, Easton and the mysterious security guard stepped in front of the ticket scalper. As if she knew what they were going to say, she quickly sang in her Jamaican Patois, *"Oh mon, she wit' yu? Sorry, mon."* She smoothly moved on to the next tourist to pitch her discount tickets to the popular island attractions.

The three headed together to the doors leading out of the airport and to the curbside pickup area. Standing there with Easton and the security guard, Andrea felt the hot breeze blowing her hair everywhere.

The heat was intense. She wondered, *What now? How are we leaving here?* She took a moment to look around and soak in the fact that they were on Jamaican soil. Easton was home! Cars, tour buses, and carrier vans rushed up to the curb, parking and blocking traffic. Travelers boarded and shuffled luggage with great anticipation of their all-inclusive vacations. She gripped her own bag tightly, aware of being in a strange place with no idea of what to expect.   The noise of planes taking off and landing was the backdrop of all the hustle and bustle. The sun beat down hard on her skin. She stood quietly, fighting her hair with her one free hand as it whipped into her face and then back out into the wind.

Two low-to-the-ground shiny black BMWs with tinted windows seemed to come out of nowhere and pulled up to the curb in front of them. The guard opened the door to the first car, and Easton pointed for Andrea to get in. With a dark leather interior, it was like a small cave. The air-conditioning met her like a cool drink. It was a relief from the hot balmy winds outside Sangster. Once they were safe in the car, the guard closed the door behind them.

The driver, dressed in summer clothes and a head full of dreads, turned around in his seat and said, *"Welcome bok boss!"*

They both extended their hands with genuine gladness as if they were old friends and shook. The driver then past a beeper to Easton. He took it, pushed the "on" button, and shoved it into his pocket.

The dread-locked driver then looked at Andrea and said, "Hello."

"Hi," she answered after looking at Easton for approval.

The driver gazed at her for a second as if he were finally looking at what he had already heard about. He suddenly whipped around and drove off from the curb. The car behind followed conspicuously close. The movement of the car grooved with a cool Reggae beat coming from the speakers. A husky Jamaican voice was singing about his dance hall queen mixed with an air horn drilled into the background of the song.

Andrea noticed that as they made their way out of Montego Bay heading to Easton's home in St. Lawrence, that his uptight posture seemed to be slowly melting away, and so were the effects of the drug in her system. She didn't want to ask Easton any questions until he was fully himself again, so she looked out the window.

Since they drove on the opposite side of the road and the streets were very narrow, she felt a little nauseous again. The road they were on had a beautiful display of what Jamaica had to offer. The sites she

135

saw were totally different from what she saw at the airport. On one side of the road were the famous, majestic Blue Mountains, which looked to have a cool cloudy mist dancing among the trees.

On the other side of the road, Andrea could see the blue waters that greeted every visitor from the air as their plane landed on the island. Every few miles, they passed through small towns where people were going about their daily lives.

The multicolored buildings flying by made her head spin. Seemingly close calls with motor scooters and bicycle riders added to her dizziness. She couldn't look away to calm her insides; everything was too exciting.

The larger homes were surrounded by low concrete walls topped with iron gates, which in most cases matched the color of the house. On the busier strips of roadway, she could hear snippets of Jamaican music pouring out of tiny cars zipping in and out of traffic. Huge resort buses also crowded the small roads, plowing through the tiny towns and leaving a trail of black exhaust smoke. Their lumbering motion rocked the tourists inside to the rhythm of Jamaica. In between towns, a strange mix of houses and shacks lined the dusty roads. Andrea saw stray dogs and even a goat or two tied to trees, all while riding in an expensive BMW. It felt strange.

The people, the ocean, and the vegetation along with the music and culture she observed from the car felt right. Andrea couldn't believe how comfortable she was in this foreign country. She decided she would be fine here. Easton's life would be her life.

Exhausted and tired of riding, she accidentally fell asleep. Easton pulled her close to him without waking her and laid her head on his lap. With one arm over her, he continued staring out of his window.

· 14 ·

FRENCH FOR DOORS

Andrea woke just as they arrived at a gatehouse. The man guarding the gate recognized the cars and had opened the gate so the cars didn't have to completely stop. The driver slowed down enough to roll down the dark tinted window to give the guardsmen a thank you nod. He then hit the gas hard to start the climb up a beautifully landscaped hill. After winding up the hill for some time on a paved driveway, they came to a two-story villa-style home surrounded by lush tropical trees and plants. This was Easton's estate, a white house with Spanish-style rounded arches along the sides of the underpass for the cars. Terracotta stone pavers led in every direction on the property. The open-air carport had enough space for parked cars and for a drop-off area in front of the house. Cars could pass through and circle around to head back down the hill as well.

Once the BMWs halted under the cover of the underpass, people seemed to get out of every door. Easton, Andrea, and their driver stepped out of their BMW first. Then, three other dread-headed men got out of the second black BMW that had been behind them. Andrea stood next to the car trying to gather her hair back into a ponytail to fix her ragged look.

Easton walked over to one of the men from the other car and gripped his hand in a brotherly shake and then a close pull-in, with their arms in between them, and gave him a loud pat on his back. Easton spoke in a friendly way to him, and it appeared he was giving the man a thank you of sorts.

Easton turned to the dread-headed driver of their car and said, *"Do yah ting now bradda. I go out 'bout ten o'clock."*

Suddenly, three tall black and brown Doberman Pinschers ran towards Easton and greeted him by jumping and circling his legs. Andrea was frightened but stood completely still, hoping they wouldn't attack her after greeting their master. Easton rubbed their heads and patted their coats. He held his hand up with his palm forward, and the dogs sat in unison with their eyes fixed on him. He walked toward Andrea, and they didn't move. He took her hand and led her to the dogs. She was reluctant to move but allowed him to lead her over.

"Hold your hand down like this, palm down below their mouth, and let them smell it."

Easton held her hand out that way and pulled it to the dogs. All three dogs smelled her hand until they were satisfied and then began to lick it.

"See, they like you."

"I'm scared of them, East!"

"Don't be. They won't hurt you."

"Are you ever gonna leave me in the house alone with them?"

He continued to pet them while they sat next to his feet.

"Nope, they're not pets. They're working. They stay outside and run free on the property. When you are out here, they will most likely ignore you from now on. I run with them on the beach for exercise, but we don't play with them."

Easton snapped his fingers to get the dogs' attention and then pointed his finger down the driveway. The security dogs took off running. Then, he took hold of Andrea's hand again, and they walked toward the front door of the house. It was rounded at the top with a very modern ornate wooden border. He opened the unlocked door, swooped her up in his arms with almost one motion, and carried her in. Though exhausted, Andrea managed a giggle. Easton stepped down into the sunken living room and spun her around to show her the space. His home was modern and very masculine. The décor was dark reds, browns, and black with a hint of white and beige strategically placed. The floors were cherry wood. The large U-shaped sectional couch took up most of the living room. It was plush and could seat several people.

"This is the living room. Over there is the kitchen," he said as he nodded toward the open flow kitchen with frosted glass inserts in white cabinets and marble countertops.

Then he nodded to the other end of the floor. "That's a guest bathroom."

Andrea could see a formal dining room across from the kitchen. Easton walked the entire lower level holding her in his arms. He then walked across the floor to double French doors with two dozen windows through which you could see straight to the ocean. The doors were huge. They were a major focal point on the lower level of the

141

house. Easton was able to open them while still holding her. Right outside was the patio area and a large patch of green grass surrounded by tropical trees and plants. Beyond that was the main event, the show stopper. The sun was leaving for the day, but she could see the blue Jamaican Ocean meet the white sands of Easton's private beach. This was his Jamaica in all its glory. The sunset was breathtaking.

Easton spun her around, still cradling her in his arms, and headed up the dark cherry wood staircase. At the top, he went to the first door in front of the upper landing. He pushed open the master bedroom door with his foot and took her in. The room was almost dark with the vertical blinds casting stripes across his king-sized bed draped with a dark fluffy comforter. He didn't turn on any lights, but she could see with what daylight was left coming through the blinds.

The bed was made to perfection just like at The Grand Mirage. The carpet was dark and plush. The room's walls had dark wood panels. The headboard was leather and went halfway up the wall. Andrea liked the masculine feel of the room and smiled at Easton's taste.

Easton laid her on his bed, knowing she was absolutely drained. It was almost 6 o'clock, and night was approaching. He took off her shoes and helped her undress. She then laid back down on the fluffy bed. She rubbed the top of his head while he was kneeling by her side of the bed taking off his shoes. Once they were off, with his hands clasped, still kneeling like he was about to pray, he sighed deeply and dropped his head.

"We're here safe and sound," she reassured him.

Without saying anything in return, he disrobed. The setting sun's stripes reflected across his nude body. She patted the bed next to her. He slowly slid into bed and pulled her into his arms. Finally, he felt real relief and was able to relax knowing she was safe. He had successfully brought what he found in the U.S. home.

Easton kissed her and gently pulled a stray curl from her face that had again escaped her ponytail. The two were covered in sunset stripes as they made love for the first time in their Jamaica, in St. Lawrence, at Hunter's Bay.

· 15 ·

MENDING FENCES

Three hours of sleep didn't feel like enough, but Easton had to get up. When he started shuffling around the room, he woke Andrea. She could hear a shower running somewhere close. She watched as his chocolate body made its way from the master bathroom to a walk-in closet and then disappear. He returned to the bed with a suit, shoes, and a tie. She sat up immediately.

"Where you going?"

"Big man tings," he answered.

"What does that mean, in English?" she shouted.

While spreading the suit out across the bottom of the bed, he answered her in standard American English. "I have to take care of business. Now that I'm back on the island, I have to get back to business. Everything's fine baby, but this is my business. I will be gone mostly at night, but you're safe here. You are alone in the house, but my house is covered. No worries for you to have. You feel ok?"

"Yeah, I feel much better now."

"Good. This is your house, so make yourself comfortable. Find some food in the kitchen. Tomorrow, we'll go shopping and buy you anything and everything you need. But tonight I must work."

He bent down to kiss her forehead then went towards the running shower. After the door had been closed for several minutes, Andrea hopped out of the bed and headed towards the bathroom.

There he was in a massive wall-to-wall stone shower with showerheads coming from every direction, all meeting up against his body. She stepped in and melted into the hot steam with him. His slippery soapy arms encircled her body and pulled her into his. He had the steam spout on that poured white steam and took all the air from the bathroom. Not being able to breathe adequately in the steam and being completely overstimulated with Easton's continuous desire for her, she took the deepest breaths she could. He told her how happy he was, and she realized her decision to leave the U.S. was a good one. She had her 10-carat diamond ring back on and could see its sparkle even through the soap and steam. This was natural and right, she thought, while taking in all of Easton and that moment.

The two black BMWs pulled up to the underpass at 9:50 pm. Easton put the finishing touches on his already well-groomed appearance. With a tiny brush, he smoothed his facial hair into place, shaping it into slim sideburns and a perfect goatee.

Easton's personal barber showed up right after his shower with Andrea. There was a one story bungalow at the back of the property that mimicked the main house in structure and style. Its blacked-out windows hid what was inside. Easton headed to that building in a casual designer sweat suit and black leather flip-flops. There, his barber met him to cut his hair and shape his beard. Andrea watched from the bedroom window, which faced that part of the property and the ocean. She saw Easton bid his barber goodbye and head back to the main house.

He was soon dressed and smelling like a man with good taste. Andrea admired him from across the room. They walked together to the front door. She kissed him deeply and tried to prolong their goodbye. After reminding him of what awaited him when he returned, she asked him when he'd be back. She was smoothing out his suit jacket and tie while he opened the door. He leaned backwards, kissed her on the cheek, and said, "*Soon come.*"

With an eyebrow raised, Andrea said, "I read in one of your brochures that, when a Jamaican says *soon come,* it basically means nothing. It said that the term is totally subjective! Soon probably means something different to me than it means to you, East."

With a big grim showing his white teeth, he realized he wouldn't be able to say that to her again and not be held to a time.

"When I say it to you, it means I will be where you are sooner rather than later! You understand that one, right? It's what you Americans like to say!"

"Sure, sure, Mr. Graham. I will expect you home sooner rather than later, like in a few hours."

Easton nodded in agreement and stepped out of the front door. He was greeted by his main driver and the three other guys from the airport drive standing around by the cars. Easton could command the men who worked for him with just one look. The look said, *let's move.*

The door was opened for him to get into the first car. After he was in, all the other car doors slammed shut one after the other. The two car motorcade moved forward around the circled driveway and down the hill past the guarded gate.

Easton's cars arrived at his boss' estate. Once through the set of checkpoints leading to the big house, the cars parked, and everyone got out. Easton buttoned his suit jacket and checked his cuff links. Another man in a suit greeted him at the front door. There was no friendly handshake. Instead, they gave each other a respectful nod. Easton knew the drill and followed the man around the side of the house to a door that led down into an area that appeared to be a basement. It was actually a fully finished separate part of the house in which to conduct business.

As Easton walked in, several well-dressed men stood up from brown leather sofas and chairs in the dark room. The hand shaking began, and the men proceeded to an adjacent large office. Everyone took their seats. Easton was now among his peers.

Seated at a custom-made broad desk was their boss, King Louie the second. King Louie was a small old man with light-skin and thick silky hair that was tapered perfectly to the nape of his neck. He was a mixture of the different races that made up Jamaica's history. You could see a little of each in him: Chinese, Indian, African, and

European. Since he was an older man, his hair was dyed regularly to its former dark brown hue. His age was not considered a weakness. He had built his empire and made more money than any of the men under his command could imagine for themselves.

King Louie the first, his father, was also in the Life, but fell way short of making boss. He was just a soldier, not even at the same leader status as the men who sat in that room. King Louie II was the Don and not to be underestimated. He was still one of the most powerful men in Jamaica. His business reached into several countries, and he was known and respected internationally. Once he began to talk, the meeting commenced. He spoke Jamaican Patois or broken English with a very heavy accent. King Louie requested explanations, and men answered with equally thick accents. Everyone was brought up to speed on business earnings in Kingston, Miami, Baltimore, and London.

Each man in the room was a leader who commanded his own separate group of men. Under them were men they called their soldiers. The soldiers handled movements of large quantities of drugs and guns. They managed the street dealers and paid side people who helped with information or with making matters go smoothly or go away.

Everyone there was vital to the operation and didn't handle anything physically that could land them on a criminal case. They all came up through the ranks and earned their spots as leaders.

King Louie looked directly at Easton.

"What yu say 'bout New York and Boston? Yu two weeks holdin' dem up, yah?"

Easton responded in his thickest accent, which naturally flowed when he talked to other Jamaicans. *"Every ting on point, boss. Delay here and dear but bok on track. Business was taken kear of. Italians make good on di deal. Rodrick will go on bok to make sure, now dat mi meet wit' di boss dear in New York. Crew in Boston satisfactory. Connection secure."*

King Louie's eyes moved from Easton as if satisfied with his explanation for the trip and the delay, so the others would be too. New orders were given, and bundles of cash were passed to each man.

After the meeting, the men talked among themselves as they drank from crystal highball glasses. When the social drinking was officially over, they slowly headed to the door where they were rejoined by their drivers and security men. Easton followed the exiting crowd, placed his glass down on a table he was passing and was moving towards the door. Then a man stepped up to him and whispered in his ear that King Louie wanted him to stay behind. Easton picked his glass back up, returned to the boss' office, and took the seat closest to the desk. The door to the office was shut quietly by an anonymous handler. King Louie was still seated behind his desk.

"I want yu to stay bok, talk wit' me 'bout yu delay in the U.S. I hear dis 'bout a woman."

Easton shook his head from side to side as if this accusation was all wrong and way off.

King Louie continued, *"Yah, I hear from di Browns yu in love in di U.S. Yu forget 'bout business, yu forget 'bout schedule, yu forget about ... "* He paused. *"Santi."*

Easton started, *"Dis true, I wit new woman. Dis serious, but I don't forget 'bout business, never. Yu taught me betta dan dat. Di Browns jest mad cause I no want Santi."*

King Louie got up from his laid-back position in his leather desk chair and walked around to perch on the corner of the desk, about to give some fatherly advice.

"I don't kear 'bout yu no want Santi, but I kear bout how dis ting getting out of hand. Dear was a way to do this ting here. Speak to Santi first, betta for business. What happin' if dis new woman don't stay here? You bok wit Santi?"

"No boss. Serious I say. She here wit' me to stay. I marry her tomorrow. Di Browns not say who I can marry!" Easton screwed up his face as he said, *"Santi jest business. Drea will be mi wife, respect. Dey will have to respect. She here wit' me, my house, MY WIFE!"*

Seeing his protégé defend the American woman and his actions surrounding her troubled King Louie. He knew that Easton was in love and in too deep with her. He knew the Browns would take it as bad business.

The Brown brothers were identical twins in their 40s, Norris and Morris Brown. Norris was the older twin by a few minutes and acted as such. Morris was known as Number Two. They were tall and big men with a large presence. They had low perfectly cut Afros with not a hair out of place. Their facial features were very African and resembled the statues and artwork of warriors you could easily see and buy around the island. The Browns had a reputation for being street thugs, especially the younger twin Morris. Some suspected and talked about mental illness being a Brown family trait. King Louie knew they could be unpredictable, but he didn't have a problem with them because they always came to him with respect and made him good money.

The Browns were Easton's equals. They were both at the meeting but kept a low profile, only answering what King Louie asked of them as it related to their activities. They felt cheated when Easton became King Louie's number two man without the official title. When Easton was a teen, he ran street drugs for the Browns. They saw the potential in him and put him in place to become one of their top men, but King Louie saw the same thing in Easton. He knew he was ripe for the picking because he had no family, no males in his life, and just an old aunt who was done trying to raise him. Because he had no sons of his own, King Louie immediately took Easton from the Browns.

The twins had been angry about that for years but wouldn't come out against King Louie because he was the Don and they needed to continue to do business. Since Easton knew the Browns like family, he was often used as a go-between to conduct business for King Louie with them. The Browns didn't take kindly to the implication of Easton being their boss.

The brothers had a plan to get around what they saw coming, which was Easton being made underboss and eventually boss when King Louie decided to give up the throne or died. They did everything they could to make sure Santianna Brown, their niece, the next Mrs. Easton Graham.

Similar to Italian crime families, Jamaican crime culture had families intertwined in the business; therefore, it was a good strategic move on the Browns' part to get their niece into Easton's bed. Now that Easton had brought this American woman back to Jamaica, he had upset their plan, and the Brown Camp had been in turmoil since the word got back he was in love in Boston. They were now saying that he had disrespected their niece, but the real problem was that they had no more moves.

Santianna was a dark-skinned, thick, curvy young woman with Chinese straight black hair down her back and bangs flat across her forehead. Her eyes slanted at the corners over her high cheekbones. Her body was perfect like that of a dance hall girl who could wind it up and put every man watching into a trance. She was raised like a princess and spoiled in every way, but she catered to Easton because she genuinely loved him. She loved everything about him and desperately wanted to be in his favor. She held the line where he wanted it and stayed where he put her as it pertained to their relationship. She was certain it was a matter of time before he married her. She would get her man, and her family would hold a higher, more secure position in the organization. Easton saw Santi regularly but treated her like a girlfriend who could and would be replaced, even though she sported a ring he gave her for her birthday on her left hand.

King Louie slid off the corner of the desk to make his way back to his chair, sighing as he walked. Easton took noticed of the slow moving bones of his godfather and recognized that he was getting visibly older. The boss sat down and leaned back in his chair while looking Easton in the eyes.

"I know all 'bout this woman. Will her modder and fadder come lookin' for her? You tink bout that?"

Easton tried to explain, but King Louie held up his hand to stop him from talking.

"Next ting I say to yu is, yu have dis woman here illegally. Yu gonna marry her illegally? I hear 'bout every move yu made wit' dis woman in Boston. So much time yu spent bein' wit' her. Yu lost yu self, boi." There was silence between them.

"I knew yu would make it bok but to what damage here, yu know? Yu didn't tink clear, boi. Yu could leave her dear and keep her a reason to be in Boston like di odder girls. I don't kear dat yu love her or stay wit her when yu go to di U.S., but when yu jack mi business for a woman yu should be replaced. Next ting now I say to yu, di Browns not gone settle for dis, day make it 'bout Santi, not business. Why I must step in here? For an American woman?"

King Louie's voice raised slightly on the words, American woman. Easton held his hands in the shape of a diamond in front of his face with his eyes cast down. He was taking his lumps. He knew he put his boss and more importantly his godfather in a bad position over Andrea. His boss was right and knew all along that he was choosing Andrea. He never loved any women except his mother and Auntie and was out of himself when it came to Andrea. He couldn't let her go. She gave him something he couldn't buy or pay any woman to fulfill in him. He knew he was smart enough to have both his business and the woman who could give him the family he never had. If he could bring King Louie around and get his blessing, he would have pulled this whole thing off with just a scuff on his reputation.

After King Louie finished talking, Easton gave him a look of respect and apology before he spoke.

"KL, tank yu for having faith in me from di beginning. I never let yu down, ever. I don't mean to bring dis mess wit di Browns to your door. I was just tryin' to get what yu have, what so many odders have in dear life. Yah, I do love her. I squared away with her mamma and daddie. She here of her own free will. She love me bok so good KL, I kayant pass it top mon. Men in dis business have women by dear side to balance dis here life and if dey blessed by Jah dey have good women to love dem after dealin' wit dem mean streets. I find dat in Drea. We are men dat get what we want right, all di time, right? I want her, I get her, I bring her bok. The only problem now, di Browns and dear feelins. Business not suffer at tall. Only ting that change, Easton is happy now with the blessin' of a woman. I fix it with di Browns someway, but I marry Drea tomorrow wit your blessing only."

King Louie began to understand Easton's need and his total blindsided emotion for this woman because it was always lacking in his life. Against his better judgment and for fear he would lose Easton all together, he took a deep breath and spoke.

"Easton, yu like my son, so I talk different wit yu. I want for yu to be able to sit right here someday, ready for dis seat. I need to know yu can make decisions based on business, not on emotion. Ya here? I want for yu what you want, son. You have mi blessin'. Congratulations to yu boat. Goan then..... marry, be happy.

Easton released a quiet breath of relief. Both men stood. King Louie walked around the desk towards Easton and put his hand on his shoulder as a sign of approval as they walked towards the door together.

"Bring her round to meet and get friendship wit the rest of the women. Not easy doe. She is American this one, but try for adjustment sake."

"I will KL."

King Louie in his usual dismissal statement said, *"Tank yu."*

· 16 ·

FOREVER

At 1:00 am Easton returned home and eased into his now filled bed with the intent to spoon naked with Andrea for the rest of the morning, but she woke and turned over towards him. She smelled like the Juniper Breeze body oils she found in his bathroom.

"Well, that was soon," she whispered.

"When I tell you something, I mean it."

"How did it go?"

"It went good. Big man *tings*, remember? I can't talk to you about my business. You just continue to make me happy and let me do what I do," he whispered back.

She felt slighted. She thought deeply about what he was saying. *Was I just told I won't be a confidant when it comes to that part of his life? That would be different… but in comparison to what? Being the wife of a lawyer?* she

159

pondered. Evan wanted her every step of the way while he built his career and their life together. Easton already had everything, a home, cars, money, and now her. How was she going to keep him happy? *He needs nothing from me except sex.* She wondered, *How long can I make his heart pound with the mere sight of me?* She was troubled by the conference she was having in her head. Easton held her tightly, rubbing her body as they spooned. His hands told her she still made not only his heart but other parts of his body pound. Between the love moans they were making, he quietly said, "We marry tomorrow at sunset." Kissing the back of her neck, he continued, "Right here down by the water."

Andrea managed a simple, "Yes"

Easton spent the next day shuffling around, making the plans for their wedding that night. He made the decision to marry her quickly, while meeting with King Louie, because he wanted to shut down any more bad feelings about his American woman. She was not his whore or a girlfriend. She was to be his wife, and that called for the utmost respect. Andrea didn't get to go shopping for food and clothes as promised. Instead, she was getting married! Easton was doing all the planning by phone, sending people all over St. Lawrence to get things to make his wedding the way he wanted. He had boutiques bring in dresses and shoes for private showings at the house. Caterers brought hot trays and cold platters. Gorgeous flowers made their way to the beach. A white tent was erected next to the patio. A portable dance floor baked in the hot Jamaican sun. Long white candles on tall silver stands were everywhere and made a trail down to the beach. Easton made phone calls to a small group of people to extend an invitation. He invited important people who would bring their wives, so they could see Andrea and she could be introduced formally.

Andrea picked a simple white fitted strapless sweetheart-top dress with crystal beading accents. Instead of a veil, she chose three white flowers from one of the groupings that arrived at the house. She swept her hair to one side, twisted it into a horizontal roll under her right ear, and affixed the flowers on top of the roll. To her surprise, the jeweler delivered three inch dangling platinum diamond earrings. She squealed in delight when she opened Easton's gift. Strappy four inch white designer shoes where laid next to the dress on the bed. She did nothing to make the wedding happen except to pick her dress and shoes. She was amazed that all of this was taking place so fast. She didn't have time to find a nail salon to put her acrylic nails back together, so she just popped them off and went with clean short natural nails.

Before putting on her wedding dress, she took a moment to let it sink in. She was sad that her father wasn't there and didn't even know she was getting married. Her plan was to, at some point, tell her father that she met Easton while working at a resort and married him. Then she would say that she was staying in Jamaica for good, of course, with her new husband.

Someone knocked on the bedroom door. She hoped it wasn't Easton; she didn't want to be seen until they met down by the beach. To make sure he didn't see her, she sent him to get dressed in his bungalow in the back, which he called the Clubhouse. She cracked the door to see who it was. A big dark-skinned woman with a jolly face in a busy floral dress with an elastic waistband was standing there. She opened the door all the way, and the woman handed her the most beautiful bouquet of white tropical flowers with a splash of pink small pedaled flowers tied with a white silk ribbon.

"Oh, thank you so much," Andrea said in a gracious tone.

"Ya welcome. I'm Miss. Merri. Easton's housekeepa and cook. Easton sent mi ta bring you deese."

"Miss. Merri, thank you so much. It's nice to meet you."

Miss. Merri nodded politely and made her way back to the staircase to be seated for the wedding.

Now dressed, Andrea took one last look in the mirror and was pleased with what Easton made available to her in such a short time. The sweetheart-topped dress hugged her figure smoothly and then kicked out into a flare at the bottom with a small train in the back. Her makeup was soft and light. She used brown eyeliner and brown mascara instead of black. Her hair was behaving for now because she hadn't exposed it to the humidity yet. The earrings from Easton were a perfect match. They swayed and sparkled in her ears.

It was time. She was ready to meet her groom down at the beach. She made her way through the house alone. She stood at the French doors and followed the tall white candles that lit the way. The sun was gently setting, casting pinks, oranges and yellows across the sky. It was perfect. A cast of unknown people in white chairs stood up and turned around to watch her wedding walk to her groom. Flowers, candles, and white Tiki torches were everywhere. There was a 10-piece orchestra seated and playing softly and beautifully as she made her way down the terracotta stone path. Easton beaming and more handsome than she had ever seen him. No words could describe how wonderful he looked in his black tuxedo, which seemed glued to his body by an expert tailor.

Suddenly, the paver stones dropped off to give way to the sand, and her four-inch heels sank with her next step, which threw her off balance. She caught herself before falling into the sand and before Easton could get to her. In another split second, he would have been by her side trying to catch her. He stopped his mad dash effort in its tracks when she caught hold of herself. She bent down and unbuckled her shoes and left them in the sand. The music never stopped even when the guests gasped at her stumble. She picked up the bottom corner of her dress, which was now dragging excessively, and continued down the sand to her groom. The fear on his face had turned back to bliss.

When she reached the decorated floral archway, she took Easton's hand and gently stepped up onto a white wooden platform. Every part of her sparkled from the diamonds dangling from her ears to the beading on her dress, to her eyes as she looked at Easton. She looked perfect and felt as pretty as she imagined she would on her wedding day. The orchestra ended the music softly so the minister could start.

"You look…" is all Easton could say while shaking his head in disbelief that he was standing in front of his bride. He never imagined this for himself. This was it. He had it all. Andrea looked out at the ocean, the flickering candles, the amazing flowers, and the magic Easton created. It snatched her breath away, and she fought back tears for a few seconds but they flowed anyway. One tear fell and dropped off her face, and a second followed. Her lips quivered, and Easton wiped each cheek with his thumb.

He leaned over and kissed her neck, saying, "It's alright to cry. Let it happen. We're getting married."

He stood straight again and rubbed her free hand with his to soothe her. He gave the minister a nod to start. His accent was so thick she didn't understand a word he said except Tamara Williams. It felt official and filled with loving words of their commitment.

At some point, everyone looked at her, so she quickly said, "I do." After a few more words from the minister, Easton said, "I will, forever."

The minister handed her and Easton the rings Easton had given him earlier. She placed a thick platinum diamond band on Easton's ring finger, and he nestled a matching smaller version up against her

10-carat engagement ring. It was a perfect fit. The minister said some more words of love, but, before he could finish, Easton dove, with a supernatural quickness, towards Andrea. He grabbed her face with both his hands and kissed her deeply. The crowd stood to their feet and applauded.

· 17 ·

THE MORNING AFTER

Still in her wedding dress, draped over a chair, Andrea tried to wake up. She was squinting from the sunlight beaming on her face through an open window. She was in a bedroom in the house she had not even seen yet. She sat up fully in the chair and checked for her jewelry. Both earrings were still on, and both wedding rings were giving off sparkles on her wedding finger. She stumbled over to a mirror and saw only half of her hair was still clipped in the side roll. Her wedding dress was half unzipped and ripped and had spots of dirt on it.

She looked around the room, disoriented and with a banging headache. She headed toward a bathroom she saw across the unfamiliar room. After rounding the corner of the bed there, on the floor she saw Easton, still tuxed up and lying face down. She could

167

hear him snoring, so she knew he was ok. She dropped to her knees and tried to roll him over. She startled him awake, and he grabbed her hard, not realizing where he was or what was going on. He too had a hangover and couldn't remember how he ended up on the floor.

"Jesus, Drea! You scared me, girl!"

She uncovered her face, which she'd been hiding to shield herself from an expected punch after Easton grabbed her. Instead, she received kisses from her husband. They helped each other up and onto the bed and tried to get a hold of themselves. Lying side by side on their backs, they stared at the ceiling.

"What happened, East? Oh, God," she said with her hands now holding her head. His fly was unzipped with his underwear poking out.

"It's always new wit yu, girl!" He tried to chuckle through the pounding going on in his head.

"Don't you remember last night, Drea? We danced, and we drank a lot of liquor. You and I did that together!" He had a pleasing smile on his face as he told the story of how they got in the guest bedroom. "We were the only drunk people at our wedding." Still smiling and trying to remember, he closed his eyes and continued.

"People started to go at the end, but we just continued to dance and drink 'til it was just us out there baby. We got in the hammock and fell straight out onto the dirt." He tried to laugh. "I carried you up *dem* steps," he continued as he pointed in the direction of the staircase outside the bedroom door. "*Yah mon,* I got confused and came to this room thinking it was our room. I couldn't go no further, so we just stayed here. We made love, darlin', with our wedding clothes ON!" He was able to laugh this time. "*Right over dear!*" He pointed again, now to a corner on the other side of the room where she woke up.

"*I rip yu dress and I keep mi suit on. Right....*" Another pause. "*Over dear!*"

He laughed again at his own tale of drunken sex with his wife. Andrea couldn't help but laugh too at the way he was telling her what happened.

"I think you're still drunk," she said with a scratchy voice. Now she was putting together her own details of what happened. She remembered that she had the wedding of her dreams with people she didn't even know. Her night was perfect because she and Easton shut the world out, got married, and danced into their marriage. She rolled on top of him and laid her head on his chest. They both stopped talking and closed their eyes. That was the best they could do until the room

stopped spinning.

· 18 ·

THE NEXT CHAPTER

Life was good, and there was no adjustment for Andrea. She fit right into Easton's life, and they carried on like they were back in her dorm enjoying each other.

Easton was with her most of the time. He would be with her wherever she needed to go. She stocked her closet with designer dresses and shoes and added to her jewelry collection. She bought some furniture and art for the house, making it slightly her own. She knew she had time to completely redecorate it the way she wanted, but for now she just made minor changes.

She was treated like the wife of a successful businessman with gifts, flowers, dinners, and shows out. Easton handled some of his business during the day now, with phone calls and quick meetings out back in his clubhouse. No one who was coming to see him about business ever had to be in the main house. He had a full office out back, which included a lounge area with a TV, pool table, and bar. It was equipped with a bathroom and a closet, so he could shower and dress out there when needed. Occasionally, there was a fierce game of Dominos with his security guards in his personal space. He stopped them from coming inside the main house now that Andrea was there. They stood in the underpass section of the driveway near the front door, sometimes talking and joking with each other. They would tap on the door to let Easton know they were there if he was scheduled to go out. When Andrea went out on occasion, without Easton, the guards would go with her and treat her with the utmost respect. Whenever she was outside around the property and came near them, they straightened their posture, hid any blunts they were smoking behind their backs, and spoke pleasantly to her. Easton had been right about the dogs; they ignored her. Sometimes she would walk slowly past the clubhouse when he had his men in there. She often overheard their conversations and tried to figure out what was going on, since Easton wouldn't tell her anything pertaining to his criminal activity. She wanted to know what he was dealing with so she could cater to his stress and his moods.

One day, she heard pieces of their conversation as she stood pretending to tighten the ties on her halter top, standing next to a blacked-out window. Easton was saying something about not wanting bodies coming out of the situation. Another man said that Heroine and Ecstasy were going into London. Bored and frustrated by not being able to piece whole sentences together, she moved on.

She wanted to know what was in the garage on the other end of the property, so she went to peek. She entered and found a normal looking garage filled with the usual items. She saw tools, golf clubs, a kayak, a motorcycle, and older beach chairs with a matching beach umbrella. Then she noticed something very large with a tarp like cover. She could see car wheels peeking out from underneath the tarp. She peeled back the front of the cover and saw the double R emblem. She pulled the cover three quarters back to get a good look at the car. It was a beautiful, shiny white convertible Rolls-Royce.

"Oh, what a beauty," Andrea said aloud to herself. She ran her hand across the hood, admiring how luxurious it was. The door wasn't locked, so she sat inside. It still smelled new. She looked in the glove box and found paperwork from when it was shipped by ocean freight to Jamaica. The car was in fact new and had hardly been driven. She got out and quietly closed the door. She gently folded the cover back over the car and continued her exploration through the rest of the garage. Nothing turned up that was as exciting as the 1988 Corniche Convertible Rolls-Royce. She knew there would be more of interest in Easton's clubhouse, but she didn't dare snoop in that space. She knew her limits and wanted him to know she knew how to be a good wife and stay in her place.

Andrea and Miss. Merri got along well planning and preparing meals together. Miss. Merri took her under her wing and taught her how to make traditional Jamaican meals. She showed her which spices were basics and how to make the popular Jamaican Rum Punch that Andrea requested. Andrea made sure that Miss. Merri was privately driven to run house errands and home when she was done working for them. Miss. Merri would always say before she left on errands *"Soon Come"* which Andrea knew meant absolutely nothing. When Miss. Merri was out on errands, time stopped. But Andrea took good care of Miss. Merri despite her time issues and made sure she was paid well. Easton was good to her, but, before Andrea moved in, he wasn't there most of the time. As a result, he didn't know how she was getting home and often forgot to leave her pay in the house. When Miss. Merri was not teaching or going over the list of house chores with Andrea, she went about running the house alone as she always had.

Andrea filled her days enjoying her private beach in the back yard and even entertained a few of the wives who did give her the time of day. She lunched with a small group of them, often at the finest restaurants in Kingston. Most of the wives were not interested in Andrea, but that didn't matter to her at all because she was almost at the top of the food chain and would soon be the top wife. She knew that then they would be running to her for friendship for the sake of their husbands' positions. Only a few were smart enough to see ahead and be friendly now.

Andrea shopped like a wife of a boss should. She had more bathing suits, kitten heels, and matching cover-ups than she could ever use. Even though she was usually out on the beach alone, she made sure she looked good. There were plenty of designer shops like Cartier, Gucci, Fendi, and Louis Vuitton on the island.

A few nights a week, Easton suited up and left around 10:00 pm. On those late nights, he would be home within a few hours. He no longer hung out with King Louie's other men as he had before. When he was dating Santi, he would frequent the dance halls, bars, and strip clubs. Occasionally, he would take up with other women. He didn't hide it. It was expected, and though the Brown brothers would see it, they knew it was what men in that life did. If Santi heard or saw anything, she would never have a say. She was expected to look the other way, and she did. She could never get upset over a cheap woman from a club. She had more on the line, with their relationship, than just the relationship. She was sure she would eventually be Easton's wife, living in his house and getting respect from King Louie's crew and her uncles. On those late nights however, Easton had been coming straight home after his meetings to slide into bed with his wife. He liked his new role as husband, and he wore his wedding band with pride.

· 19 ·

NEW WOMAN NEW PROBLEMS

Andrea was excited about going with Easton on a trip across the county to the well-known Half Moon Golf Resort for a retreat of sorts with his partners and their wives. King Louie would be social and partake in the festivities with his wife for the three day trip.

LV brown-leather bags sprawled all over the master bedroom were evidence that Andrea had been on a shopping spree and now was on a packing spree for the trip. She was packing for herself and for Easton. She wasn't sure what to bring or what jewelry to take, since Mrs. Louie the second would be in attendance, so she packed as much as she could.

"East," she yelled from the top stair rail to the lower floor.

"Yah," he answered.

"Your golf clubs are in the garage? Are you going to golf while you're there?"

"*Yah, I'll get dem and send dem to di car,*" he half yelled back.

His attention was on the piece of mail he'd found lying on the kitchen counter. He didn't notice the fact that Andrea knew he had golf clubs because he was preoccupied with the envelope. He figured Miss. Merri must have brought it in with her. The envelope was addressed to him but had no return address. Most mail that came to the house was junk mail because his address was not public. He had no need for mail because what he needed was sent by courier service under a different name. He wondered how this got into his private box, so he was half listening to his wife.

He unfolded the sheet of paper that was inside the envelope and pictures fell out onto the kitchen floor. He picked up the pictures and looked at them first before reading the note. They were pictures of Andrea lying out on their private beach with no bikini top on trying to tan her breast. He couldn't believe Andrea took her top off outside.

Immediately, anger washed over him. His mind was racing trying to figure out who took the pictures and how far the person was from his wife. It had to be someone using a high-powered lens because his property was not accessible and was guarded by people that Andrea didn't know were there. He also wondered where the dogs were. He quickly moved to the next picture, which was of him and Andrea walking hand-in-hand in a straw market enjoying a day shopping. The next photo was from their wedding. It was of them taking their first dance as all their guests looked on. The last photo was of the pair coming out of The Grand Mirage in Boston. He flipped back to the note as his anger was building by the second. His jaw was clenched so tight you could see the outline of his jawbone.

The note read:

YU TINK YU CAN DO ME DIS WAY? I HAD A PROMISE THAT YU BROKE.

YU TOOK MI EVERY WAY YU WANT ON A PROMISE THAT I WOULD BE WIT YU. YU PROMISE MI UNCLES SO THEY LET YU HAVE ME JEST TO EMBARRASS MI BY MORE DAN CHEATIN IN DI STATES.

I CLOSE MI EYE SO MANY TIMES HERE AND DEAR 'CAUSE I DON'T WORRY 'BOUT SEX. EVEN JEST SEX IN DI STATES OK BY MI, BUT YU DO THAT TING SO WRONG. YU NOT CHEAT, YU BUY HER! RISK EVERY TING HERE FOR HER. YU BRING HER BOK HERE AND FORGET 'BOUT MI.

NO TALK WIT MI OR MI UNCLES AND YU MARRY HER! YU LOVE HER IN ONE MEETIN', BOI? HOW DIS BE? YU NEVER LOVE MI, RIGHT? AMERICAN

YU WANTED ALL DIS TIME, HUH? YU NOT GET AWAY WIT DI SHAME YU CAUSE MI.

NOW I PROMISE YU!

Santianna Brown was beyond angry. He quickly took the pictures and the note and headed out to the clubhouse to put them away.

Andrea had only been out there a few times when no one was there except him. She understood that was the place where he commanded his crew and was off limits, so he didn't worry that she would find the pictures. She would come out when he was working alone to entice him inside the main house for food or to give her some attention. He didn't have a problem with her snooping in his business, so he took the envelope to the clubhouse.

After running the situation over again in his mind, he calmed down. He knew he'd have to now work in a meeting between himself and the Browns during the Half Moon retreat since they would be there too. He had assumed the Brown Camp had accepted that he was married now and had not even thought about Santi, since he didn't hear anything more about it.

He couldn't let this be a problem for King Louie. He had to end this matter so that they would force Santi to move on. The ring he gave her didn't mean anything because he didn't ask her to marry him. He just gave the woman he was sleeping with a ring for her finger, any finger, on her birthday.

He knew Santi would be upset and hurt when she found about Andrea because she wanted to be more to him, but he never expected this kind of drama. Easton couldn't believe the Santi situation was still spilling over into business and causing so much trouble.

"Neither the Brown Brothers or Santi will cause me, and certainly not my Drea any more drama," he mumbled to himself while entering his clubhouse.

After he tucked the disturbing letter and photos away, he got his golf clubs from the garage and took them to the waiting limousine so his driver could make room for them.

The drive to Montego Bay would be long, and he wanted to ride with his beautiful wife in comfort and style. The LV-stamped brown bags were being squeezed into the trunk as he came around the corner with his clubs. Shaking his head at all the luggage, Easton knew Andrea was enjoying this.

· 20 ·

HALF MOON

Andrea had not been in a limousine since they left the States. Extreme comfort, champagne, Reggae music playing throughout the car, and Easton's lap to lay across for the long drive were nice.

He was back to staring out the window with concern all over his face but continuously rubbed her hair spread out over his lap. His BMW followed behind the limousine with three of his guys in it.

She tapped his chin with her finger from underneath him to break his stare. He tilted his head down to look at her as she lay across his lap.

"You alright?" he questioned her.

"Yah, mon. I just want to know what 'tis worrin' ya, my sweet boi?" she said in a Jamaican accent. He couldn't help but smile at her attempt to copy his sometimes accent.

"Nothing for ya to worry ya pretty head 'bout," he responded.

She sat up and kissed his lips and said softly.

"Dat's what gets me so excited, boi, when ya talkin' to mi like dis!"

Grinning, he looked past her to the see where his driver's eyes were and then told her, *"Don't be startin' no ting right in here dat get yu in trouble, gal."* They laughed together, and his troubled mind relaxed.

They arrived like stars at the Half Moon Resort. The staff was excellent and extremely accommodating. Their suite looked like old money with classic furniture and décor. A schedule of private banquets, drinks at the bars, shopping trips, and beautiful ocean-front golf games for the fellas were laid out on paper at the dining table in their suite. A welcome basket of fruit and champagne were next to it.

Andrea wondered if the staff knew how many gangsters they had on the property for these days. The gun power alone was a frightening thought. Fortunately, all attendees worked under King Louie, and there would be no problems, especially here.

Andrea was introduced to King Louie and his wife at the first dinner. She and Easton sat at the Don's table, which made her feel elite and special. Mrs. King Louie was cordial enough but not overly friendly. She noticed the green-eyed monster present in some of the wives because she was "that American woman" sitting at the head table. Every wife was adorned with jewels and wore beautiful evening gowns.

The only words explaining why they were all there came from King Louie as he raised his champagne glass to the private room full of people and said, *"To di fruits of our labor!"*

In unison, everyone in the room said, *"Hey!"* and raised their glasses for a toast.

It was a lovely evening of socializing with old partners and getting introduced to new people. Andrea made it to all the shopping trips and lunch gatherings with the ladies, which she enjoyed. Easton spent time at the bar with some men laughing and talking sports. He attended the afternoon of golf on the internationally known course at the ocean's edge. There was no business talk. The retreat was purely social, so the men could feel connected to people they didn't always see. It served as a reminder that they were all under the same boss.

Before Andrea knew it, the retreat was over. They had attended the last formal dinner banquet and were heading down the hall to their room to pack. Her mermaid gown had long fluffy material at the bottom that floated around his and her legs as they walked. Easton informed her that they would stay a little later into the evening even though everyone else was checking out and leaving. He explained that he needed to have one more meeting. The truth was that he didn't want the boss to catch wind of the problem with the Browns, so he asked to meet with them well after the others were gone.

Leaving Andrea to pack, he worked his way to the Browns' suite to settle the matter of Santi and the message he received. Norris Brown the older twin opened the door. They greeted each other with a tux-to-tux hug. They had all been at the last dinner party of the retreat and were still dressed.

"Come in, bradda," the first Brown said. Number Two Brown was not as free with the brotherly love. Easton knew the first brother better and understood that the second was more of a hothead. He ignored Number Two's stiffness and walked into the suite. He unbuttoned his tux jacket and sat at the head seat of their dining table.

185

"*Marriage done yu well, bradda,*" the first Brown brother complimented.

"*Yah, mon. I'm happy for sure,*" Easton said. Before Easton could say anything else, the first Brown brother started with a reminder.

"*Yah know we go far bok, right? Yah jest a wee boi when we put yu ta work?*"

"*Yah, yu right 'bout dat.*" Easton had to agree to move the conversation along.

"*Yu know dat I will always look after yah business interest. I never see yu wit no inside or a take,*" Easton responded playing his game. Brown Number Two took a seat at the table next to his brother with no words, just a nod to Easton.

Easton continued. "*I come to yu braddas as a bradda wit a matter dat need to be settle wit us. Now dat yu know ya business is secure and I don't forget no ting and I see dat yah paper keep moving to yah houses, I need di matter of Santi taken kear of. She steppin' outside of proper ways and causin' me trouble in mi house. She screamin' mad. I kayant have dis no how. Apologies, braddas for any disappointment mi cause her, but I never proposed to her.*"

The first Brown brother, Norris, was now feeling backed into a corner, since Easton was crafty about having this sit-down and assuring them he would keep their money flowing.

186

Norris leaned back in his chair, trying to shift his strategy, and said, *"Yah mon, Santi vexed and runnin' mad about dis ting."*

He blew air from his lips and shook his head, as if he couldn't figure out why Easton didn't marry his niece. He continued, *"Ya could have had Santi and the American too, bradda. I would have made it ok wit Santi, as long as she was the wife. You broke promise wit us."*

Easton also leaned further back in his chair now. *"I make no promise to yu. This Santi ting was good for yu, not me. I don't need ally wit yu. I just told yu I take care of yu under KL, so what now da problem?"*

"Take Santi as girlfriend now. Dat make us happy."

Now Easton was even angrier than he was about having to meet with the Browns. He had to process the suggestion of taking Santi as a girlfriend to keep the peace!

Easton replied, *"Dis mean yu don't trust mi word, Brown. Dis mi life I choose. Clear yu brain of this wit Santi."* Easton, being done at that point with the meeting, gave instructions.

"Here what yu do for sake of peace. Handle Santi, make sure she make no more troubles for mi, and I make sure no troubles for yu."

With that, he stood up, buttoned his tux jacket, and walked out of the door, leaving them sitting at the table.

Once on the other side of the closed door, he could hear Brown Number Two speaking in a loud raging voice.

"I no speak to have peace! Dear be no peace!" Number Two's voice got even louder with his next statement. *"He make yu to be a sketel slut!"* he shouted.

Easton knew he was shouting at Santi now. She had been there hiding and listening. As Easton walked back to his suite, he couldn't believe this situation was not going away. It didn't go the way he wanted, but he hoped they heard him loud and clear that he was next to the Don and their disrespect wouldn't be tolerated, no matter how far back they went. His problem now was to make sure King Louie didn't get word of the dissention over the "American woman."

Easton's handsome tuxedoed form rounded every corner of the hallways with the smoothness and style of a strong black man. He replayed their request of keeping Santi as a girlfriend to make them comfortable. He couldn't believe this was about his loyalty to them, and that his word meant nothing. What they were asking for was not ever going to happen.

· 21 ·

BREACH

Andrea was still wearing her evening gown, but was all packed up when Easton returned to the suite. She was ready to get the car loaded so they could start the long ride home. While walking arm-in-arm with her husband through the hotel heading to the parking lot, she took the opportunity to ask about the symbol of wealth covered up in the garage.

"Tell me something handsome man of mine."

"Yes, what does my wife need from me now?" he answered while he fished around in the tuxedo's breast pocket for the Cuban cigar he didn't have a chance to smoke earlier in the evening.

"Why are you hiding that beautiful car in the garage? I went to look for a larger beach umbrella and found that you are hiding a Rolls-Royce!"

They stop walking for a second. Easton cut the tip of his cigar and lit it. After his first puff, he held his arm out for her to again loop onto, and they continued walking to the waiting cars.

"I'm not hiding it, baby. That's where I park it. You like it, huh?"

"Oh, it's beautiful," she said with glee. "Why don't we drive it?"

"I bought it because I saw one in the States and thought it was the ultimate ride for a man of my position," he joked while puffing smoke. "It's too much. It brings way too much attention. But we can take it out sometimes. I'll drive you myself."

"What? You can actually drive?" she teased.

"Yes, woman, I can drive! We'll take an evening ride with the top down… just you and me."

"You mean with no dread-heads following us in the BMW?" They both laughed at her nickname for his security guards.

The parking lot was dark, and men were shuffling the multiple pieces of luggage around trying to make them fit in the trunk of the limo as they had in the driveway of the house before they left. She could see that Easton's golf clubs didn't make the cut and were being placed in the trunk of the BMW instead.

Once Easton and Andrea reached the cars, she decided to head towards the open limousine door by herself. She would wait there for the guards to finish loading the cars and give Easton joking time with them while he finished his cigar since he was in that kind of mood.

She gestured to Easton by nodding her head to the side towards the open door to let him know where she was going. He grabbed her hand with the hand that was not holding the cigar to help her and her gown step inside.

In a split second, screaming could be heard coming from behind the limousine and heading straight for Easton and Andrea by the open car door! Andrea was one second away from stepping into the back seat when they were both hit with a rushing force!

Someone was running and screaming towards them when all four of Easton's guards jumped on the running figure, creating a snowball effect of bodies flying through the air. When Easton and his bride were hit with the rush of four men and an unknown assailant, they were both smashed into the open limousine door. There was a loud bashing sound followed by a cracking noise. It sounded as if there's been a car accident in the parking lot of the resort.

Since Andrea was on the end of the thrust, she took the hit of six people crashing into her, which pushed her into the open car door. When the snowball of bodies came to a final stop, everyone who had been standing was now either sprawled out on the pavement or in the pile with the assailant who was still screaming underneath the heap.

It all seemed to happen in slow motion for Easton. He couldn't stop the running people heading straight for him, so he turned to grab his wife. Instead, he hit her as they hit him. Andrea's body hit the limo's open door and then her head met the blacktop like a professional fighter hitting the mat after a knockout. Easton landed on top of her, while Santianna Brown was on top of him with a few guards on top of her.

Easton struggled with all his might to reduce the weight on Andrea. Growling with clenched teeth, he did a push-up over Andrea's body, holding everyone on top of him on his back! The weight was getting lighter as the guards one by one made it to their feet. With all the confusion, Santi was able to free her arms to reach from the pile to pound Easton on his head and about his back with her fists while she screamed unrecognizable words of anger. Easton couldn't block the

192

blows because his hands were holding himself up over his wife with bodies still on his back. Andrea lay limp under him.

Within seconds, Santi had taken her revenge. A professional hit man wouldn't have been able to pull off an attack in the presence of Easton's security the way she had. Easton was praying to God that Santi didn't have a knife because he didn't have a hand free to grab her arms.

The confusion came to an end when guards finally grabbed Santi while she was still laying on Easton's back. But she could no longer take swings at him. Santi was screaming that she had a ring too. Every other word between screaming about the engagement ring that Easton gave her was littered with a mixture of Jamaican and American cussing. Within a few more seconds, Easton's men brutally snatched Santi off of his back.

As soon as he was free of her and the pressure of the men holding her down, he in one incredible swift movement was on his feet and at Santi's throat up against the side of the limousine. Her screaming rage came to an immediate halt once Easton had his hands around her throat.

The men who were supposed to protect Easton panicked and went from holding her to trying to manage him, who was choking the life out of her and slamming her repeatedly against the side of the limo. His teeth were clenched so tightly that the veins were popping out in his neck and forehead.

Once they realized he wasn't going to be talked into releasing his grip on her, they physically pried him off of her, fearing he was really going to kill her. They knew he reacted without thinking because his wife was hit, but they also knew who Santianna Brown was and that this was going to blow up even worse if he killed her.

Santi fell to the ground gasping for air and trying to cough, but she couldn't. Being held back by his men, Easton said nothing. His eyes were fixed on Santi's slumped body on the ground heaving.

"Boss, come bok! Get yah mind right, boss! Look at me boss!" said the guard holding him on his left side. The guard holding Easton on his right side just held on tight and kept his head down.

"Boss, come on, mon!. Come bok! We gotta go!"

Easton took his eyes off the first woman he had ever put his hands on, and he relaxed his muscles to show his men he was in control. They slowly released him. He was breathing heavily and trying hard to stay in control. The guard who was talking to him knew he had snapped.

"Look, go to yu wife. She's hurt. We take this crazy girl from here. We gotta go!" the guard shouted.

It was as if he forgot what sent him into the rage. His head snapped around to see Andrea lying in the street next to the broken limousine door. Glass was shattered all around her and was in her hair and face. When he scooped her up, he saw blood. Feeling all over her, he found the source of the blood in the back of her head. Three of Easton's guards dragged Santi away while he tried to rouse Andrea. He held the gash on the back of her head trying to stop the bleeding.

"Boss, we gotta go. Dear are cameras, and security will be out here soon. We kayant have the Browns out here tryin' to settle dis now. We go to di hospital straight away!"

Easton knew he really had to move now. He stood and fully picked Andrea up in his arms. Her long flowing evening gown fell loose all around her, exposing her legs. He sat as far as he could from the broken door in the limo with Andrea on his lap. The car door was hanging crookedly, half on the car with the hinges now bent out of their functioning shape.

Three guards took off in the BMW with Santi in it and sped out of the parking lot. The guard left who had brought Easton back around was trying to get his boss out of what could be a more dangerous situation if the staff alerted the JCF police or if the Browns appeared. He tried to kick the door off its broken hinges to no avail. He then pulled his gun and strategically shot both hinges off, firing as far away from the car as he could. When the door finally fell to the pavement, he threw it inside the limo. The guard then ran around the car to the open trunk and slammed it shut. He jumped into the driver's seat and hit the gas at the same time. The wind was rushing through the hole where the door should be.

Easton couldn't believe this had happened at the hands of a woman. He had witnessed death, people killed, and torture in the streets, but never had someone he loved been hurt because of him. He couldn't get his mind to accept that this happened right before his eyes. His men didn't protect him, and he wasn't able to protect his wife.

It was dangerous for them to speed down the dark roads in the tourist parts of Montego Bay where the speed limits were low. Easton was gently picking tiny pieces of glass from Andrea's face and hair. He needed to release the emotional pain he was feeling, but he couldn't.

196

He didn't know how to calm himself, because he had never felt the kind of rage he was feeling. All he could do was concentrate on Andrea in his arms, hurt.

The wind from the missing door woke Andrea. She began to cry with her eyes closed. He kept calling her name, but she wouldn't open her eyes. She just cried softly.

"Drea!" he called loud while holding her face under her chin. "Open your eyes, baby! Open your eyes for me!"

She slowly opened her eyes to a squint and stopped crying. "Thank you," he said in a whisper to God.

Now that she was awake and not crying, he had to rethink the hospital. He didn't have her fake passport or any ID to get her medical care. They were more than two hours away from St. Lawrence where he had doctors on his payroll. He was willing to risk the hospital visit and her deportation if he had to, but she was now awake.

"Talk to me, baby. Where are you? What's your name?"

"You pushed me. You hurt me," she said in the softest voice.

The thought of her thinking he would hurt her in any way pained him terribly.

"No, no, baby! I wouldn't hurt you never. We were attacked, and I fell on you. We were hit by a crazy person. You were just on the bottom of the pile, baby. You alright?"

He went back to, "What's your name?"

Slowly she was coming around. "Mrs. Easton Graham." She managed a small smile only to reassure him. She knew he was distraught and that he was trying to hold it together. She never wanted to see him in pain as much as he didn't want to see her in pain. She was trying extremely hard to rally herself so her husband could calm down. With only one of her eyes open now, she told him she would be okay.

"You think you can make it all the way back to the house to see my doctor? I got no papers for the hospital, and you know what that means."

"Take me home," she mumbled, turning her face into his tux jacket and trying to stop the pain in her head by shifting positions.

She then realized he was holding the wound on the back of her head with his hand, and her shifting made the pain worse. Easton leaned his head up to speak to his guard who was maneuvering the dark narrow streets with the enormous car.

"We go home instead. Can we make it with' no door?" Easton shouted!

"Yah, mon. When we stop, if we have any problems, take care of it," he said while passing his gun over his shoulder to Easton. Easton laid his hand with the gun in it across Andrea's hip aimed at the open door in case someone wanted to jump in through the open door when they had to slow down or come to a full stop. What he knew was that anyone trying to enter the car would have their own gun. Easton planned to pull Andrea as close to his chest as he could with his left arm and be the first to shoot with his right hand, if even one foot of a stranger entered the hole in the car.

The ride was long and gave Easton time to hear whispers in his head telling him that Andrea was a mistake. He heard words that encouraged him to just let go and take his frustrations out on the Browns or anyone who tried to get in his way. He heard another whisper tell him he was too wrapped up in her. The voice said that he selfishly put her in harm's way. Another voice, almost overlapping the prior thought, said that he loved her too much and his business would suffer and they both would end up dead.

199

The couple of hours it took to arrive in Hunter's Bay felt like all night to him. But they pulled up the hill and made it to the underpass with a missing door and no carjacking incident.

A feeling of relief washed over Easton first, followed by an overwhelming feeling of blame. The back of Andrea's head was starting to clot which was good. Easton gathered her and her dress up and carried her into the house with his guard in tow. He laid her down on the large sectional couch in the living room, while his guard was on the phone calling the doctor, Dr. Crisp. After the call, his guard gathered ice in a kitchen towel for Andrea's head.

Easton kept the lights down low and placed the icepack on the back of Andrea's head. She winced and kept pulling the ice away. He knelt on the floor in front of her body just watching her. He whipped off his tuxedo jacket and threw it down as if it had been restraining him all night.

"Boss, Dr. Crisp on di way."

"Tank you, Sean."

For the first time, Andrea heard Easton address a guard by name. She repeated his name to herself. "Sean."

Dr. Crisp arrived in no time and to Andrea's surprise, the doctor was a woman! She was a light-skinned very attractive woman in her late 50s, Andrea guessed.

Dr. Crisp gave her eight stitches, an antibiotic, and pain medication. She determined that Andrea would be fine with rest and proper removal of the stitches when the wound healed.

As Easton walked the doctor to the door she looked at him with suspicion surrounding Andrea's injury, but said nothing. Easton gently handed her a cash tip for giving him the news he wanted to hear. Dr. Crisp was paid to see nothing and know nothing when taking care of anyone Easton called her for. But, this case was a woman and gave the doctor pause even though she was told Andrea fell in a parking lot after tripping on her dress. Dr. Crisp controlled her emotions, took her tip, and thanked Easton on her way out the door.

After Easton gave Andrea the medication and put her to bed, the three other guards arrived at Hunter's Bay. He called a meeting with the guards in the kitchen. This was the first time they had been inside the house since Andrea arrived. They often had been back and forth through the home's lower level before the house had a mistress.

In his bloody white shirt, Easton paced back and forth rubbing the back of his neck before saying to the four men, *"What di hell happen out dear? How dis happen now?"* He threw both his hands up in the air in disgust.

"I was jumped by a woman while I'm wit' mi wife, wit' all four of yu dear!"

No one said anything because they knew Sean as the head guard would do the speaking when ready. The three guards under Sean were nervous. They knew that the boss and his wife were ambushed while they stood right there, and somebody had to pay. Sean was nervous too because he knew the gravity of what had happened, what he let happen. A part of him knew the kind of man Easton was. He had been with Easton long enough to know his style and knew him to dispense violence only if necessary and even then it was business and with a clear head.

But ever since Easton returned from the U.S. with this woman, he had been different, so Sean wanted to make sure Easton didn't do something uncharacteristic standing in the kitchen.

Sean's mind assessed the entire situation, while Easton kept asking the same questions about what happened in several different ways. Sean knew that Easton hadn't handled being with this American woman correctly from the start. He knew that his boss's feelings for her were out of control. There was no doubt in Sean's mind that the night's events shouldn't have happened, and the obvious disrespect needed to be taken care of; but his boss hadn't thought any of his actions through. Easton was not making good decisions, especially about bringing this woman to the island.

Easton continued at almost a shout, *"If that was a bad boi wit a gun, he shoot mi, den mi woman be still on di street bleedin'! Dis should never have happen!"*

While Easton's rant went on, Sean concluded that Easton was just blowing off steam and wouldn't be punishing him or his crew for what happened.

Sean continued to assess Easton in his mind. If Easton was in fact losing his grip because of this woman, he knew his boss was wide open for a fall. *A fall was usually in the future for these guys at the top anyway,* he thought, *but not over a woman.* Certain that no guns would be pulled in the kitchen that night, Sean began to talk.

"Boss, we know dis real bad for yu. Look, di path was clear before yu come out di hotel. She be waiting in a car for yu. We saw a woman approaching wit no suspicion. It happen so fast, mon. It good ting we not shoot her. Tink bout that."

203

He continued, *"Yah know for sure no bad boi make it to you, ever, wit out shoot me first. Dis a woman, a woman of di Browns'. Dis different case. We handled the best way. She not hurt. She jest mad. Deese guys say when dey take her for a drive to calm her, she never talked. She jest look mad. She was taken bok to Half Moon and put in her car. She drive away to go home."*

Easton leaned against the refrigerator door and put his hands in his pant pockets, still looking sharp even in a bloody dress shirt with missing cuff links and a hanging bow tie.

"Yah, yah, Sean. I know dis bad, but yu did di best ting. Tank yu for pulling me together, mon."

Easton was now talking in a quieter tone. He then shook Sean's hand unexpectedly and bid them all good night. The four left the house. Two stood first watch in the driveway, and two slept in the BMW in shifts, securing the house.

Easton had never been backed into a corner like this. He had heard the talk that was going around about him that he was gone over this woman, but he ignored it. The pass King Louie gave to his MIA stunt in Boston made the men continue to grumble, fueled by the Browns. He was not the Don yet, so he wasn't given the total respect he wanted.

Easton climbed the staircase, worn out from both the initial stress of dealing with the Browns and the high-powered adrenaline that shot through his body in the parking lot of the resort. He felt drained because of worry over Andrea and exhausted from his angry outbursts. He climbed into their bed on top of the covers with all his clothes still on. He had already tucked Andrea into bed after the doctor finished with her. She was now sleeping deeply. He had nothing more to give and no energy to get undressed. He scooted himself into a spoon position next to her. He couldn't get close enough in his mind. He held her with only one arm so not to disturb her. Finally, his muscles began to relax and let him go to sleep.

· 22 ·

QUESTIONS AND ANSWERS

As sunlight began to peek under the closed vertical blinds in their bedroom, Easton showered and got dressed. He put on a black designer velour sweat suit with black leather sandals and headed down to his clubhouse before Andrea woke from the awful night before.

When she finally opened her eyes much later in the morning, he was already returning from the clubhouse, where he'd taken care of some business. He was carrying a breakfast tray filled with ackee and saltfish, steamed callaloo, scrambled eggs, bacon, watermelon wedges, and her cup of coffee. She could see the important part of the tray coming her way, the steaming cup of Blue Mountain Coffee. She had learned to cook all the items on the Jamaican breakfast plate with Miss. Merri's guidance but preferred not to eat ackee and saltfish with callaloo for breakfast. She preferred them for lunch or dinner. Black Americans traditionally ate fish and greens at those times and not at breakfast. She had become fond of the coffee and had it every morning without fail.

She noticed his designer sweat suit, which she had never seen him wear before. Still holding the breakfast tray, he did a balancing act trying to kick off his sandals so he could climb into bed with her while she ate the mounds of food Miss. Merri made.

"Can you eat?" he questioned.

A small scratchy sound came from her lips. "Yeah, I'm a little hungry."

She sat up against the leather headboard holding her head with both hands trying to stop the pain coming from every direction.

"Where does it hurt?"

"Everywhere!"

He put the tray across her lap and climbed in next to her. He reached for her pills left by Dr. Crisp. He opened the top, spilled out two pills, and handed them to her. Gently he leaned her shoulders forward and pulled back the bandage covering her stitches to see how bad it was. He was reluctant to tell her that that a patch of her hair had been shaved to make way for the eight stitches. He covered it back up, and she went straight for her Blue Mountain cup of coffee.

Easton knew the conversation was coming as soon as Andrea swallowed her pills and had enough coffee to organize her thoughts. He leaned back against the headboard too and waited for her questions. She daintily picked at the scrambled eggs with her fingers and ate just a few fluffy pieces before the noise of Miss. Merri vacuuming across the hall broke the silence.

"Easton," she said without moving her eyes from her plate while she picked now at the bacon. "What happened? Why would that woman want to hurt you, hurt me?"

Andrea had managed to put some pieces of the event together and remembered what the crazed woman was screaming before she was knocked into the car door and to the ground.

"Drea, Santianna Brown is her name. We all can't figure out why or even how she did that. She's the niece of very close business partners of mine. I was involved with her, but it wasn't serious. I made the mistake of going along with the appearance of a deeper relationship with her for the sake of business. It was easy to date her because I didn't have anyone else in my life. Unfortunately, I didn't handle it well.

When I met you, I never gave her a thought. It was insensitive on my part. Now feelings are damaged across their whole family. I never thought in a million years that she would attack me or hurt you. I am going to deal with this mess."

He looked her straight in her face and beckoned her eyes to meet his directly. "I promise you on everything I am that I will never let you get hurt again. I'm so sorry, and I feel such pain that I failed to protect you. Forgive me," he begged, while placing his right hand over his heart.

She reached out and stroked the side of his face and said, "I understand. I'm fine now, and I know you'll handle this."

The room was silent again until they heard Miss. Merri outside the closed bedroom door gathering the ripped bloody evening dress along with Easton's destroyed tuxedo. He had placed the ruined clothes outside of the bedroom door for her to dispose of.

"Are you going out tonight?" she asked.

"No. I talked with KL already and told him I'll be at his place tomorrow night and that I needed to stay here today and tonight to make sure you are ok."

She was so glad that she would have him all to herself all day and all night. With his explanation and apology, she felt comfortable and fully understood what happened. He on the other hand felt no better than the night before, but she didn't have to know his deep concerns and what was on his plate to deal with. He was home with Andrea, but his mind was working trying to figure out his strategy for the Browns and for getting King Louie to back him up, with the least amount of drama. Even though he was number two, he never took his position for granted and knew King Louie did not like the petty infighting that affected business. He would have to walk carefully with his boss even though he was clearly in the right.

After a few more hours of sleep, Andrea struggled to get out of bed and headed to the shower. As soon as the bathroom door closed behind her, she heard Miss. Merri in the bedroom pulling sheets and collecting the breakfast dishes. The multidirectional showerheads shot out with force as she turned the knobs on.

Before her shower, she leaned over the sink to see how bad she looked. She was not surprised to see that she looked as bad as she felt. She confirmed that she in fact did look like she was hit by a truck, but a truck in the form of a crazy person.

As the mirror started to fog, she also noticed her eyes were beginning to blacken. She gently pulled down the skin under each eye, but that didn't stop the blood that was pooling from giving her two black eyes. She moved on to the wound dressing on the back of her head and ran her fingers over the stitching. She realized her hair had been shaved and worried for a moment about her appearance. She always wanted to look like that girl Easton fell in love with. She had to keep her position. She knew that not only was this crazy Santianna person waiting to unseat her, but there were plenty others who weren't crazy. She had to keep it all together no matter what happened. Because she had lots of hair and her natural curls were thick, she would be able to cover the spot. She promised herself she'd mend quickly so she could be available for her man in every way.

· 23 ·

DAMAGE CONTROL

Easton's routine of getting ready for a meeting at the boss's house went as usual with the dressing ritual except for the kissing goodbye at the door with Andrea. This meeting would be a two-part session. Easton would talk first with King Louie, and then the Browns were scheduled to join them.

After being escorted to King Louie's underground office, Easton calmly told his boss what had happened. He only became emotional when sharing the detail about his wife's eyes being blackened by this disrespect from Santi, which was allowed by the Browns. Easton never mentioned the meeting he'd had at the Half Moon with the brothers after everyone had gone. He stuck to the facts of Santi and the ambush that could have brought attention to their presence at the resort, which could have led to a possible shakedown from the police being paid to keep things quiet. The government didn't tolerate any unsavory activity in the tourist areas because of the money that flowed there from foreigners. No bad press about crime could come out of these areas. Those were the facts that moved King Louie in the direction Easton wanted.

Knowing that the Browns would come into the sit-down trying to make a deal that would get Santi back into his bed, Easton made sure the ruling was made before they entered.

King Louie agreed that action was needed for the Browns; therefore, he agreed to a penalty that satisfied Easton.

The Brown brothers arrived and unbeknownst to them, decisions had already been made regarding the situation. They would have no opportunity to negotiate terms of any kind. King Louie spoke direct and with very little emotion.

"This ting dat happen yu know no good for business. A mess with a silly women dis is. My problem here is di attention yu bring to mi business and of course di disrespect."

After that setup, he went on to inform the brothers that he was pulling from them several illegal holdings they'd been allowed to manage and make money on and giving them to Easton. They included deals that were happening in the U.S. They would not reap any money from those deals going forward. The deals they were left with were not worth as much in comparison, but they were still money makers. The Browns were to make sure that Santi was not heard from or seen again by Easton or his wife. They were to make her understand that Easton was married, the organization recognized his marriage, and his wife would be respected. If they could not hold Santi accountable and make sure she did not contact them again, he would send her out of Jamaica to London.

King Louie concluded with, *"Tank yu,"* which was the indicator that they were dismissed and could leave.

Easton never addressed either brother with words. Brown Number Two couldn't hide his anger, it was all over his face. Easton's face showed anger too, which let them know that any allegiance to them was now really in question.

· 24 ·

A NEW NORM

Several weeks went by. After the meeting with the Browns and their boss, no one heard from Santi, and things were running smoothly. Feeling confident that the whole matter was settled, Easton began thinking ahead like a true boss. Even though he was earning more money than he ever imagined from the Browns' business, he knew that after a significant amount of time passed, he'd give back to the Browns the business they'd lost to him. He needed to pull the group of leaders back together and let the matter die, ending the bad feelings, gossip, and rumors. Easton knew for sure that he could never trust the Browns again!

Slowly, Andrea got back to herself. She no longer resembled a raccoon, and her hair had grown back where the stitches had been. Her routine of lying in the sun, shopping, and pleasing her man was back in full swing. Their life resumed with dinners out, weekend getaways, and any new thing she wanted to see or experience on the island. Easton indulged her with no questions asked.

Easton had been changed by the attack that hurt his wife. He had handled the Browns, and he was confident that everyone had accepted the ruling and the organization hadn't suffered because of the incident. But his personal life needed a change. He needed to change.

He began to pull away from Andrea. He began to move their relationship into what he thought was a normal marriage between a man in his business and his wife. He knew he could no longer be so totally in that state of extreme love for her because it put everything he worked for in jeopardy. His wife could not be his only priority. She was a part of his life, but he needed to treat her as only one part and keep his main focus on his business.

He resolved to never again be caught in the position of not thinking clearly because his feelings for his wife were out of control. Their protection depended on him being fully himself. He thought carefully about what he had to do to make those changes. He decided that a little separation from her was necessary. Needing distractions, he resumed the late nights hanging out at the strip clubs with the other men. He took his pick of girls ready to do whatever he desired. When he went out, he was now layered in extra security so he could really have a good time. He drank more than he ever had before and found that it didn't take much to fall into cheating to keep Andrea in her new place.

The love he had for her didn't change, and he still took care of her in every way. He still made her feel special when he was with her, but he spent less time at her side. He hid from her everything he was doing, outside of their beachfront home. He convinced himself that he had figured it all out and was back on his game. He believed he was becoming more and more like King Louie. He acted as if he already had the crown on his head.

Business was good, and the money flowed. There was nothing Easton couldn't buy. He had no desires and neither did his wife; therefore, he could do what men did away from their wives with no guilt. He respected his wife by not bringing any of his infidelities on or near his property. When he'd been with another woman, he never got into bed with Andrea afterward, not even just to sleep. He would go to another bedroom in the house. In his mind, he owed her that respect. One night, she found him in a spare bedroom and tried to get into the bed with him, but he refused her and walked her back to their master bedroom. Andrea never attempted to join him again when he did not come to her after being out.

Andrea was deeply wounded by Easton's pullback during the day and sleeping apart some nights. She knew that her marriage was falling apart. She thought of several possible reasons for the changes in him. Maybe he was bored with her. Maybe she was no longer able to melt away the tensions of his business life with her looks, all the attention she gave him, or even sex. Maybe he was having business related issues and needed to focus. Andrea eventually relaxed her mind and freely gave him the space he was taking without her permission.

· 25 ·

HONEY

Easton planned to go to Ocho Rios for the weekend to attend the Jamaican Jazz Festival and didn't tell Andrea about it until he was packing. Walking behind him trying not to seem upset about his trip without her, she asked question after question.

"Who are you going with? Are the wives going? None of them mentioned the festival to me."

Between each question, he planted a kiss on her lips without answering any of them, until he realized the kissing wasn't going to stop the interrogation.

"Just us men are going, that's all. Business too, you know during the time there. No worries for you. I'll be back Sunday night."

He was feeling her pain, and it was breaking him down. But he stayed strong, and walked out the door. He was keeping his new structure of business and his marriage together by making sure his feelings for his wife were in check and by enjoying the occasional tropical fruit to balance things out.

The festival was all fun and no business. It was held at one of the popular resorts in Ocho Rios. It was a time to unwind and enjoy the music, food, and good liquor. At a poolside table with several men talking trash about any and everything, Easton was enjoying himself and feeling powerful by buying rounds for large crowds of people.

Dominos, playing cards and cash littered several tables where people played games in the hot Jamaican sun. Unattached women were everywhere, looking to get into something. They were seeking out the money men. The heat, the flow of liquor, and the live background music combined to create the perfect outdoor club atmosphere for mingling and ultimately hooking up, even if only for a few hours before moving on to the next event.

Easton wasn't interested in the half-naked women who made their way to his table. He enjoyed his beer with shots of Hennessy. The other guys squeezed butts and whatever else they could get away with while flirting with the chocolate, mocha, and light-skinned luscious bodies. The liquor and the heat were getting to Easton, so he took

Sean with him to enjoy some air-conditioning in the hotel lobby bar. He didn't want to return to his room because he wasn't ready to call it a day, but he needed refreshing.

They hadn't yet made it to the bar when they saw an ideal spot to sit in the lobby. With beers in hand, they sat down. Sean sat gap legged and leaning forward with his elbows on his knees, clasping his beer in both hands as he continually surveyed the area. He conspicuously watched everyone approaching and passing. Sean couldn't be and wasn't drunk, not even buzzed, but Easton was on his way.

A front desk girl kept looking over at them, especially at Easton. Local girls knew "rude boys" when they saw them. The front desk girl knew Sean was his guard and that Easton had to be pretty high up on the criminal chain.

Sean, while still holding his lookout pose, turned to Easton, *"Desk girl want to be wit yu,"* he grinned.

Easton noticed her too. She was pretty, as most front desk agents were. She was flirting with her eyes.

"Yah," Easton answered Sean back. *"Get her for mi."*

Sean knew to make the arrangement later for the girl to find her way to Easton's suite, but for now he continued his surveillance.

221

After their cool down spell in the lobby, Easton and Sean finally moved to their original destination, the bar. It was dark and cool, with people moving about with drinks and appetizers. They sat in the corner and continued to enjoy the air-conditioning while watching the people mingle.

In came a group of woman wearing short tropical dresses with sashes draped across their bodies. High on their heads, they had crowns, with jewels that looked like diamonds. Easton couldn't make out the writing on the sashes but zeroed in on the light-skinned beauty queen with the tallest crown. Her face wasn't as made up as the other girls, and he liked that. She was a natural beauty with straight light-brown hair and hazel eyes.

The ladies moved towards the men and chose seats a few tables away but not before the hazel eyes met Easton's. All cooled down from the heat, Easton settled his tab, and he and Sean made their way across the bar to leave.

Easton decided to go to the bathroom before going back out in the heat. He and Sean followed a long hall to the men's room. On the way back, they strolled the long hall again. This time, they saw the beauty queen walking toward them. As they passed, Easton spoke in a smooth gentleman's tone. She stopped to reply. Sean continued to the end of the hall out of sight. They talked for about 10 minutes.

When they parted, Sean appeared again. Without looking at Sean as they continued their walk out of the bar, Easton said, *"Bring her to mi instead tonight. She will met yu here at 10 o'clock."* Sean grinned as he thought about what Easton was about to get into that night.

At 10 pm on the dot, the beauty queen was waiting. Sean escorted her to Easton who had rented a private tent that was staked on the beach for the evening.

She was impressed by the extra effort he'd made. She expected to have a night with him without any romance or much conversation. Easton was drunk from drinking all day at the festival but tried his best not to appear so. They continued the conversation they'd started in the hallway of the bar. They sat close to each other on the same chaise lounge, which matched the striped design of the tent.

Her name was Sasha, and she was at the Jamaican Jazz Festival with the other girls to promote a beauty pageant. She was in fact the reigning Miss. Tropical Oasis Beauty. She would be giving up the crown to a new winner soon. He noticed that she didn't have an accent or that she was not using it the way he did, alternating back and forth. She talked about herself to make him comfortable.

"My mother is from the U.S. and lives there still. My dad is Jamaican and lives here. They're divorced. I've gone back and forth throughout my childhood and just finished college in California."

He was intrigued by her because her accent was like Andrea's, and she had many of the same qualities. They didn't look alike, but they were both beautiful to him. As he scooted close to her, he smelled her perfume, which was even more intoxicating than the liquor he had been drinking.

"Every ting irie! Isn't that what us Jamaicans say all di time?" he joked.

She allowed him to approach her face without skipping a beat in their conversation. She played it cool because she wanted to rope this big fish. With guards not far away and the gangster attributes an island girl could see right away, she knew for sure that he was a kingpin.

He fell into her well designed spell. Before he knew it, he was kissing her and trying to claw his way to her bare skin. She could taste the liquor on his tongue and knew he had been drinking a lot but couldn't tell if was drunk. Her crown fell to the sand with the force of his passion.

Sasha wondered if the reason she got so close to him so quickly was because he was intoxicated. By tomorrow, he could possibly be a different person and not interested in her at all. It was a risk she was willing to take.

After their heat got to him, Easton told Sasha they should go back to his suite. Sean appeared, and he and Sasha followed Sean. Before they made it to the room, Easton and Sasha fell several times against the hallway wall kissing. At one point he had both her arms above her head with their fingers intertwined, kissing her the way he kissed Andrea. In his drunkenness, he forgot he didn't kiss anyone like he kissed his wife.

Easton picked her crown up from the hallway floor after the last stop and swung it around on his index finger as they continued to the suite. Sean opened the locked door and let the two of them go inside alone. No more talking, no more flirting. The drunken sex happened just how he intended it to.

The beauty queen stayed the night. Easton looked at her wrapped in a hotel towel after her shower sitting across the table while they ate breakfast. Wet hair and all, she was a natural beauty without a bit of makeup. She had been right, Easton was now sober and a different gangster than she met and slept with the night before. It was like starting over with her game because he wasn't drunk. She'd have to try harder to appeal to him with more than her looks.

Easton was not the groping man she met at 10 pm the night before. Now he was interested in what she had to say. He realized she had some of the same mannerisms as his American wife, trying to please her man. But she didn't talk as much as his wife; she only said what was necessary for the moment and nothing more. The similarities were a comfort to him. Sasha didn't expect much out of this tryst but was trying for a repeat of the night before. If she were lucky, she thought, maybe she would become his side woman since anything more wasn't possible with the huge platinum diamond wedding band on his finger. She ignored the ring that set the limits to what she could have with him. She did feel she had him almost in her grasp but she didn't want to push him. She wanted him to walk straight into it.

"Meet me for lunch," he asked.

She quickly agreed but suggested dinner instead to guarantee another round of "gangster sex", her name for their sexual encounter.

"I'm leaving tonight, checking out," he informed her.

Switching gears, she agreed to lunch but suggested lunch in the suite by room service.

"That'd be ok," he said with a grin, knowing he was going to get into her again. *One for the road*, he joked with himself.

Lunch turned out the way both had expected. This time, she had sex with the real Easton Graham. He wasn't clumsy or groping her like the night before. She felt the sexy strong aura that women often noticed when they were with him. He was forceful but gentle and made sure she was a part of the encounter.

While they ate lunch after, he took the opportunity to have real talk in a casual manner.

"Can I see you again? You know I'm married," he said while holding up his left hand to make her acknowledge his wedding ring.

"Yeah, I see," she answered without staring too long at it.

"I like you, and we had a good time, right?"

"Yeah, Daddy, we had a good time."

When she said "Daddy," his face made a glitch movement as if the word stung him like a bee. She noticed right away and vowed never to use that word again. She took that as a clue that this arrangement would be more than sex for money. She was not to treat him like a john.

"How about honey? Can I call you honey?"

He liked that and smiled without agreeing to the new pet name. He continued his proposition. "I'd like to see you again and maybe again and again," he chuckled. They both smiled.

"I love my wife very much and will not hurt her in anyway. Our friendship will be discreet. We are friends, and friends can have fun without hurting other people."

She got the drill and the nature of their future visits and was onboard with being whatever he was suggesting...... for now.

· 26 ·

THE MONROE AFFECT

Andrea was still steaming about Easton's trip to Ocho Rios for the jazz festival. But as usual, she worked on a plan.

She made sure that she was looking spectacular for his arrival. She had a hairdresser come to the house to set her hair on big chunky rollers for the look she had when they met. She hadn't worn her hair in large smooth flowing curls in a while. Andrea knew that hairstyle wouldn't hold up long in this humid, tropical climate. It was easy to wear it in its natural state of spongy curls. Even in her signature ponytail, her hair was playfully sexy. From the first time Easton gently played with a curl from her ponytail, she knew sitting under the hot dryer for hours wasn't necessary to look the way he liked. But today, she needed him to see what he missed by not taking her to the festival.

When the hairdresser finished, she had Marilyn Monroe shoulder-length waves instead. One side of her hair covered her dramatic smoky eye make-up. She had also found a lady who could do her French-tipped acrylic nails which she missed desperately since she was unable to get her fills anywhere in Jamaica.

With her perfectly done hair, new nails, wedding diamond earrings, and the sexiest long-sleeved, off-the-shoulder, red mini-dress, Andrea greeted her husband as he came in the door with beautiful flowers for her.

Easton was pleasantly surprised to see her in all her sophisticated glory, but he always saw her as beautiful even when she wasn't trying.

His mood was cheerful but not as excited to see her as she would have liked. The effort she put into being beautiful for him made him tingle on the inside. He held back from wrapping her up in his arms and swinging her around to show her that he loved the way she looked.

When she planted a kiss on him, she expected him to ravish her right there on the foyer floor, but he didn't.

"Baby, you look so pretty. What did I walk into here? You hiding a man? You didn't do all this for me, right?"

Crushed by what he said, she wanted to cry, but she held it together. She was losing him and didn't know how or why.

Easton saw the hurt on her face and came back with, "Oh, I'm just kiddin', baby. I missed you, and what a nice surprise to see my woman all done up for me."

She didn't feel he was sincere but she shook it off, grabbed his hand, and led him to their formal dining room.

"I planned a romantic evening for us, honey."

His face contorted slightly, like he had a twitch he couldn't control, because that sweet word of affection honey was now coming from his wife.

"Look, we have dinner," she pointed out. The whole table was laid out from end to end like it was an American Thanksgiving dinner. The candles flickered and danced to the quiet playing music in the background.

"Wow!" he shouted when he saw the romantic display. This is what he wanted, rather than him gushing over her with uncontrollable love, he let her fill the room with excitement all by herself. This was the home that bosses created and enjoyed. He would play along as she tried to rekindle his affection, but his mind was made up as to the way he would be with her. All of his affections would be given in the bedroom. There, he'd give all that she wanted. In the bedroom, he would let loose and show her the same affection she saw at the start of their relationship. This new way of being was working, he realized. Tonight, he would break his rule and go to their bed.

Easton leaned back in his chair and opened a drawer to the credenza that matched the dining room table and chairs. He pulled out a professional looking camera with a neck strap that dangled from it.

"What are you doing with that?" she asked.

"I am going to a take your picture! I only have wedding pictures of you, did you know that?" he said.

He held the camera up to his eye and starting shooting fast shots one after the other.

"Oh come on, Drea, you can give a little something. *Gimmie a sexy pose to put in mi wallet."*

They both laughed while he continued to snap shot after shot. She finally gave in and started to give him sexy poses. She posed with her hair covering her one eye and with her chin touching her shoulder, looking directly at him as sexy as she could without smiling. He shot another picture every time she held a different position. After a while, though, she started to feel silly and threw her head back to laugh. Even then, Easton kept on snapping so he could capture all of her various expressions. He wanted to enlarge one photo and hang it in his clubhouse.

Easton decided to stop embarrassing Andrea so he put his camera back in the drawer. To her relief, they went back to their romantic meal.

Across the table over their curried lobster salad appetizer, Andrea small talked Easton while feeding him from her fork.

"You see I have my own plate right here, right?" he laughed.

"I know. I just want to feed you."

"What else we got on this table to eat, woman? Did you cook all of this?" he questioned.

"Well," she said while flipping her head to one side to move the hair that covered her one eye. "I had help from Miss. Merri. It didn't take as much time as you'd think."

The truth was that she supervised while Miss. Merri made the dishes she wanted. She spent most of the day under the hair dryer, in the makeup chair, and doing everything else that put her expensive sexy look together for the evening. She continued the tour of the dishes displayed across the table, pointing them out with her fork.

"Pumpkin soup, swordfish steaks, jerk chicken over rice, scalloped potatoes, fried rice, sesame chicken wings, corn fritters, fried plantains, and for dessert rum cake with vanilla ice cream."

He sat back in his chair sipping his wine, feeling full from just seeing all the food. He went back to eating the first appetizer, the curried lobster salad. Miss. Merri tried to tell Andrea it was too much with too many different kinds of foods, but she didn't listen. Andrea wanted what she wanted.

While they were sampling the sesame chicken wings, she mentioned that she heard from one of the wives that LaTrice was back on the island. She told Easton one of the wives probing for gossip asked her if she knew LaTrice from Boston. Knowing that the woman knew the answer already, Andrea indulged her questioning so she could get information about where to find LaTrice. Easton simply said that LaTrice no longer worked for him now that she was done with school.

"We have no business with her any longer," he stiffly added.

"Oh, I just thought that… well, I really don't have any friends here. The other wives just tolerate me, which is ok for lunches and shopping, but LaTrice would be a great change."

With his mouth full and chewing, he managed to say, "I guess I don't see a problem with that, but if she gets into some other working situation, then we can't cross lines. You know what I mean."

"Oh, ok, well that makes me happy. I'll give her a call and invite her to lunch," she said with a smile.

He already knew that his organization wouldn't need LaTrice anymore and that she would probably go work for someone else if she stayed on the island. In that case, Andrea would be off limits to her. She had out lived her usefulness after what happened in Boston. He wanted their conversation to move away from LaTrice, so he got up, walked over to her, and pulled her out of her chair and back with him to his chair. He sat her on his lap and now fed her.

It had been months since he had first pushed back from her, but now she felt sure her extra efforts to romance him had done the trick. *He's back*, she thought, and gave him every bit of what he wanted from her after dinner.

· 27 ·

LATRICE

When Andrea called LaTrice she noticed that she seemed a bit cool towards her. Andrea didn't take it too seriously. She thought that maybe LaTrice was still mad about how things ended between them in Boston. She convinced herself that LaTrice would be glad to see her and to reconnect with her. Andrea had long since let go of what LaTrice did back in Boston because it all worked out for her. She had her prince. Now, she needed a friend in Jamaica, and LaTrice would be a godsend.

Andrea couldn't wait to tell LaTrice all about the life she now enjoyed in Jamaica. She wanted to tell her about the wedding and the beautiful beachfront property she called home.

Andrea made reservations for the upscale restaurant Flor Bonita inside the historic Spanish Tidwell Hotel, in Kingston. She thought LaTrice would be impressed with her choice. She counted the days until she reunited with her friend.

When Andrea arrived LaTrice was already there and seated. Andrea was escorted through the luxurious restaurant by the tall slim maître d'. She knew through word of mouth that this would be an impressive restaurant, but had never been there herself. She was indeed impressed. It featured crystal chandeliers, white-glove service, and a separate wine room that could be seen across the main dining room adjacent to the bar area. She strolled on ornate low carpet which was only in the island's most-expensive restaurants.

Once at the table in the center of a sea of other dressed-up tables, Andrea broke into a wide grin. She opened her arms to LaTrice for a huge hug. LaTrice never stood to receive her and stiffened when Andrea embraced her. Andrea pulled away and sat down in the chair the maître d' was holding back for her. Confused, she looked across the table at a LaTrice who had a very different look. She was dressed much too casual for the restaurant and now had a short haircut that wasn't becoming on her.

Andrea ignored the way LaTrice sat across from her like a hostage. She continued to act like a lady and made the best of the situation. She promised herself that, after the lunch, she would never look back again when it came to LaTrice.

With her hands folded on her lap, Andrea started talking. "Well, it's nice to see you. What have you been up to?"

LaTrice warmed enough to carry on the conversation.

"Girl, I've been just fine," she said with a sarcastic tone.

"Well, good. I was glad to hear you were back on the island. You graduated, right?"

After taking a sip of her wine, LaTrice got right to it. "Yeah, I sure did. I heard all about you and Easton, the wedding and everything. You don't have to tell me all about your good fortune; it's all over the island. Congratulations," she said flatly as she raised her glass to Andrea.

"Oh, that's interesting. My circle is small, and not too many people are interested in what I do."

Andrea casually took a sip of her wine too. Her mind raced, wondering where the conversation was going.

"Oh, yes, people are talking, Dirty Girl."

Shocked that LaTrice had the nerve to call her that again, she was going to get her straight right now!

"Excuse me?" Are you still on that? Clearly of the two of us, you are the Dirty Girl," Andrea spat back with a strong tone. Then she cocked her head to the side as if to say, now what?

"You are and always will be a Dirty Girl because you do what you do."

"Well, if I recall correctly LaTrice, you were worse than a Dirty Girl in Boston. You were, let me see..... a whore! You slept with drug dealers for money, shopping sprees, and, oh yeah, limousine rides!"

LaTrice would have never knocked another woman's hustle, but the grit of her animosity was because she felt that Andrea's hustle kept getting in the way of her hustle. That was the real problem. She couldn't believe this girl almost messed up her money in Boston when she played Easton and took him off his game. LaTrice saw it as a strategic move on Andrea's part to get more out of Easton and that she knew the full ramifications of him not conducting his business on time while with her. LaTrice then gave a clue to Andrea as to why she was still angry.

"Your circle is small but not small enough, because I am fully aware of why I no longer am welcome to make paper."

Now whispering because she realized her surroundings, LaTrice continued. "My plans were to stay in Boston, but I was told I'm no longer needed as a front. No one else will touch me now, which means I don't have work because the princess in the big house has demanded it so. Well, we all know that you have Easton by his balls, and your wish is his command!"

"Are you kidding me?" Andrea shot back in a deeper whisper, now leaning forward across the table.

"Number one, I don't tell East what to do in his business. And number two, I don't give a damn who you sleep with to make your paper. If you want to be the equivalent of a street slinger in this business, then more power to you!"

Then, leaning back in her seat, Andrea continued in a very proud tone. "I have better things to do with my day in my beachfront big house as you called it. I spend money 'til I'm satisfied, and, oh yeah, pleasing my man who makes all that possible takes up a lot of time too. My concerns are not about what you're doing, Miss. Thing. My concerns are whether my driver will get me to the lunch with the wives on time or making sure the newest Fendi purse is on its way to my front door. Those concerns come way before worrying about the pennies you are trying to make!"

Now I'm done with this chick, Andrea told herself.

LaTrice returned with, "Well, before you continue to count your money and the times you think you are pleasing your man, I have a bit of news for you."

LaTrice slid an envelope across the table. Andrea slowly picked it up and opened it. Inside was a sheet of paper with a letter in all caps and three photos.

She read the letter:

> *YU NOT RUNNING ANYTHING HERE IN JAMAICA. YAH TIME IS SHORT SISTA.*
>
> *YU MESS WIT DI WRONG PEOPLE HERE.*
>
> *YU MESS WIT MY SITUATION AND OUR MONEY. HE'S COMING BOK AND YU WILL NO LONGER HAVE A HOLD ON HIM.*
>
> *LOOK GOOD NOW. HE FOUND SOMEONE NEW!*

The first photo was of Easton at the strip club with a dancer bent over with her butt in his face and his hands on her. Her heart started to pound, but a voice in her head said, *Don't worry about that; she's a stripper. That's what men do. You can deal with this.*

The second photo showed Easton through a cheap hotel window. He was in a chair with the same stripper sitting on his lap. Now, Andrea was trying very hard to control her anger.

The third photo was of Easton groping the beauty queen in a hotel hallway against the wall. He was kissing that woman the way he kissed her when they made love!

Andrea stacked the pictures and shoved them and the note back in the envelope and into her purse. She stood without a word or a look at LaTrice and walked out of the restaurant and across the marbled floor of the hotel lobby.

Then, one of Easton's guards followed her out the door and stood on the sidewalk in front of the Tidwell Hotel with her.

"Should I get the car?" he asked, keeping a distance from her.

"No, we can walk together. Which way?" she said looking down like she was looking for something so she wouldn't cry.

He started walking towards the underground parking lot where he had parked the car himself. She walked beside him, turning and taking steps with him quickly. He hadn't used valet parking because he didn't want anyone else inside the car.

Once they reached the BMW and she was securely in the back seat, she struggled harder to keep control of her emotions.

They barreled out of the underground parking lot and headed back to the house. Twenty minutes into the ride, she broke down and cried of embarrassment and the ultimate betrayal from Easton.

The guard asked softly if she was ok, but she ignored him. She tried again to get herself under control but couldn't. She sobbed loudly, watching the tropical trees on a beautiful sunny day fly by very fast outside the car window.

· 28 ·

PROOF

Easton spent his afternoon with Sasha at a hotel that didn't compare to the Tidwell. It was one of the smaller hotels nestled in a tropical beach cove for tourists.

He made arrangements to meet her there and planned to only spend a few hours, thinking that's how long it would take for Andrea and LaTrice to have lunch. She met him at the door in a white terry cloth robe, which she opened slightly to give him a peek once he was inside the door.

The room had Caribbean décor front to back with multicolored fabric on the drapes, comforter, and chairs. It was the perfect moderate priced hotel for visitors not able to afford one of the more popular, all-inclusive, better known properties. It was far enough away from home yet not too far so that he'd be gone only a few hours.

Sasha was beautiful, but she wasn't his wife. He reminded himself that he wasn't trying to replace his wife, whom he adored, but that she was just to release some of the energy that caused him to get too wrapped up in her. It was working. He was able to keep Andrea where he needed her, so he could make better business decisions.

Without much conversation, they got to what they were there to do. He liked that Sasha knew how to handle him. She knew what this was and didn't push for anymore. He wasn't playing games with her like taking off his wedding band. He wanted to enjoy her, give her the perks for being with him, and get back to his wife. He didn't want to mess with those club women anymore. They were too much of a risk. He liked that he was dealing with one woman that he could keep from being with anyone else by paying her well and treating her special.

Easton took a hot shower afterwards with the same soap he used at home and made sure to use his regular cologne too. Sasha watched him put himself back together, noticing he was doing it too perfectly. She knew he was making sure his wife didn't see any changes in his appearance. She thought he was handsome when they first met, but she couldn't appreciate his total look without the aura he had about him when he was sober. He was a smooth dark handsome man, but the countenance of him as a boss added even more to his good looks. He was so exciting to Sasha.

As he sat in one of the very busy patterned chairs in the room, he bent over to put his shoes on. His shirt was still unbuttoned and gapping open. She watched him, she admired him, and she realized she wanted him more and more every time she saw him.

He asked, "Have you eaten? I'll wait while you shower, and we can go get something."

Sitting on the edge of the bed wrapped in one of the sheets, she responded, "Sure, honey that would be nice. I like talking to you over a meal."

"I like talking to you too, Sasha. You're different, and I like your American accent."

"Your American accent isn't too bad either," she said.

"Oh, yeah, I forgot to tell you that I spent a lot of time in the U.S., and, when I talk to you Americans, I automatically *drop mi island talk, mon!*"

She chuckled dutifully to make sure he felt that he impressed her. It was her job, and she knew all that he needed in order for her to be with him… for a while and hopefully more than a few hours a week.

"I was born here, you know. I just spent most of my life in the U.S.," she reminded him.

Easton pulled an envelope from his small travel bag and walked it over to her. "I thought you would like to buy yourself something nice. I don't know your taste, so I thought maybe you could get what you like."

She took the envelope from him and didn't open it. She just placed it in her purse. From the feel of its thickness, she knew it was more than a few bills to buy a dress or some perfume.

"Thanks, honey," she said as sultry as she could.

"No problem," he said while buttoning up his shirt.

She jumped up and headed to the shower so they could continue their date with an afternoon lunch.

There was an unexpected knock on the door. The shower had not been turned on yet, so Sasha heard it and cracked the bathroom door to see who it could be. Easton got his gun and walked to the door softly with the gun hanging low by the side of his leg. He put the chain on and cracked the door while he wondered where Sean was. Sean was standing on the other side. He closed the door back, pulled the chain off, and opened it fully. Sean didn't go in; he just started speaking quietly.

"Dear is some kinda problem with Mrs.," Sean told him.

Easton's heart dropped, though his face didn't show what he was feeling.

"What yu mean?" Easton said.

"She home now. Di lunch end already. I got beep, mi call over dear, and dey say she cry in di car."

"Let mi get mi tings," Easton told him.

Because of the haste with which Easton grabbed his travel bag, wallet, and pocket things from the dresser, Sasha knew he was upset. She closed the bathroom door just before he walked over to it.

"Sasha," he said with a tap on the door with his knuckles. She opened the door with no clothes on to try to entice him to stay. His eyes never left her face.

"I gotta go. Rain check on lunch?"

"Sure," she agreed. Without giving her a chance to say anything else, he was gone. Sasha knew for sure now that he loved his wife, and he was going to try to keep her at arm's length. She knew she had a hard road ahead of her if she was going to try to shake him loose from this wife's grip.

In the car ride back to the house, all Easton could think was that Andrea was hurt in some way or the injury she suffered at Half Moon somehow had done something to her brain that made her cry uncontrollably without telling his guy why.

When they pulled up, he saw the other BMW parking in the underpass. His BMW pulled smoothly behind it.

"*Sean, take kear of dis bag here.*" Sean knew he wanted him to put his travel bag away so Andrea couldn't find it. Easton jumped out of the car and ran through the front door. He shouted from the foyer, "Drea!" No answer.

He looked in every room, running in and out of doors. Standing in the middle of the kitchen, he noticed her on the beach facing the water still dressed from lunch and still holding her clutch purse. He opened one of the French doors and quietly headed to the beach.

When he had almost reached her, he said, "Drea, you alright?"

She turned around surprised to see him because she had been so deep in thought trying to process what had happened in Kingston with

LaTrice. She looked him in the eyes, and walked past him towards the house. She stopped in the kitchen, kicked off her shoes, and snatched her earring from her ears. He approached her slowly and tried to hold her, but she pulled quickly away and backed herself around the kitchen island so it was now between them.

"Baby, what's wrong? Are you hurt?"

"Yes, I'm hurt!" She began to cry again.

"What happened?" He was sensing that whatever was wrong was directed at him.

"What are you talking about, Drea?"

She grabbed her purse and pulled out the envelope and threw it across the island between them. As it slid across the smooth marble surface, the pictures spilled out face up and landed right in front of him. He was utterly surprised and devastated at what he saw. He couldn't believe that she saw them and he'd allowed her to be hurt again.

He picked up the pictures. The first photo in the stack was him against the wall with Sasha's arms high above her head as he kissed her. His mind swirled in a million directions trying to concoct a lie to control the situation. But, before he could pick a lie, he flipped to the next picture of him with a stripper, so he didn't bother to try lying.

Andrea was completely unhinged and sobbing. He had nothing to tell her, so he just stood there and stared at her.

After a few seconds, he threw the picture across the room with clenched teeth and made a growling noise. He walked to the French doors as if he were going out but instead began punching out the windows one by one. Glass flew everywhere, and Andrea was still crying. After all of the windows at the higher level were gone, he kicked the lower one out. The guards were close enough to observe that this was Easton breaking glass, so they kept out of his sight around the side of the house. Andrea, unmoved by his anger, turned away from him and made her way slowly up the stairs.

Once he was done destroying the doors, Easton leaned against the kitchen wall to gather his thoughts. He chose to give Andrea space. He had never seen her this distraught. When she cried back in Boston, it killed him to watch, and he promised to make sure that she never cried again, especially about him. The Half Moon incident made him a liar the first time, and now this was the second time. His plan to control his world had come crashing down again.

When he decided to head to the living room, he noticed the paper that the pictures were wrapped in, snatched it from the counter, and read it.

His anger kicked up to a thousand all over again. Thoughts came fast and furious, *LaTrice is now Santi's messenger? She has no place having beef with me. She's nothing! Who is she to get even for her lockout? She's trying to deal with me? She let the Browns convince her that I am powerless or that my time will never come? I'll have my own message for her before this night is over.*

Now that the decision about LaTrice had been settled in his mind, he moved onto thinking of how to fix his marriage. Instead of going to the living room to think, he went out the front door and whistled for his dogs. They came running from several different directions and walked with him to where Sean was standing in the driveway. He told Sean that LaTrice was to be taken care of but that he didn't want her body to be found. In his mind, there was no need to get the Browns back in a position to make complaints to KL over a nobody. He knew that the Browns saw her as a nobody too, but they would make her a somebody if they could keep KL interested in nonsense involving him. His patience with the Browns was running short, and he wasn't going to be forgiving much longer. But, he'd rather deal with them once the torch was passed to him. For now, his thinking about this new problem with the Browns was that nobody moves and nobody gets hurt, except LaTrice.

For two days, Andrea didn't speak to Easton. She spent most of her time locked in one of their many extra bedrooms. Their one year wedding anniversary had come and gone with the two of them separated from each other in every way. Easton tried a few times to enter the bedroom, but the door was locked. When she was around the house, she ignored him. She wasn't all done up trying to play the normal games to get his attention. She was serious and deeply hurt.

On the third day, Miss. Merri was in the kitchen cooking. It was her day to cook and clean for them. Andrea went down to the kitchen hoping for a good meal. After she greeted her with a gentle hug and kiss as she always had, Miss. Merri took one look at her and knew something was wrong.

"*What wrong wit yu, child?*" she asked her with concern all over her round face. "*Yu not sick, huh?*"

"No Miss. Merri. I'm ok… just tired."

"Sit, sit," Miss Merri commanded. Miss. Merri brought over a cup of bush tea and sat it in front of Andrea.

"What wrong now?"

Andrea attempted to lie but just couldn't. She pulled a worn out tissue from her sleeve and dabbed the corners of her eyes before the tears started. To her surprise, none came. She figured she had none left. She began with a deep breath. "My husband is cheating on me."

Miss. Merri felt completely relieved but tried to look surprised. She rubbed Andrea's shoulder before responding to her deep hurt.

"Well, mi darlin, mi sorry for yu hurt, but yu know dis be with dis kinda man you marry. He be a powerful man and wit power come choice to take up wit different womens. I tell you di truth, he love yu more dan yu tink. Yu know what dey say around 'bout him? Dey say him "gaan to bed" wit that American gal! Yu know what dis mean? That he so in love wit yu, him not tink bout dem important tings he do in dem streets to make dis money."

"Miss. Merri, we had something different I thought. I came here, leaving everything and everybody for him because he was mine and I was his."

"I know this hard for a gal like yu to understand, but listen. I know him from a boi. I know him Auntie. Him a good man and don't want to hurt yu. It jest a part of dis life, di life yu want. Yu di Mrs. Dem sketels-sluts want ta be Mrs. Yu di Mrs. Stay di Mrs!"

After sharing her wisdom, Miss. Merri kissed Andrea on the forehead and went back to stirring her pot of ox tail stew. Andrea waited for a bowl of the aromatic dish before thanking Miss. Merri and returning to her new room. She left the door unlocked and cracked.

A few hours later, she heard Easton come in, make his way to where the ox tail stew was, and start talking with Miss. Merri. The patois they were speaking was too deep and too fast for her to understand. About an hour later, she heard Miss. Merri head out and get in one of the BMWs out front. Just as she thought he would, Easton crept through her door, trying to gauge her mood. He dragged a chair across the carpet to sit next to the bed, so he could face her while she was lying against the headboard. He didn't attempt to touch her, even though everything inside him yearned to hold her and make it better.

"Baby," he spoke. She looked at him, her eyes full of sorrow.

"I'm sorry you had to see those pictures. I never wanted to hurt you. You are my wife."

"Our marriage isn't legal, East."

"What?" He couldn't believe what she was saying. "Well, no, but that's not because I didn't want to commit to you. You're here illegally. When I'm in the States, I'm there illegally. So there is nowhere we can

255

get a marriage license with both of our real names on it. YOU ARE MY WIFE!" he said sternly. He was offended by her mentioning that fact. "Let somebody try to tell me different and they have a problem, Drea!"

Silenced by his affirmation of their love, she just sat looking at him with her arms folded.

"There are some things that I just can't explain to you, Drea. This life is different than a life you would have had with an American man with a regular straight job back home. I have to be who I am and all that goes with that. You need to know and fully understand that no one, I mean no one, comes before you. You need me, and I'm there. You can't be replaced, ever. Anybody else is just game for a minute, and I am always safe. I promise. I need you to be the wife of a man in this position and be secure in your place. Your place is here," he said as he grabbed her hand and placed it on his heart.

Andrea leaned her whole body into him and laid her head in his neck. He whispered, "I'm sorry, and I will never have another woman cross your path."

· 29 ·

NEWS

Andrea couldn't believe the cards she had been dealt with Easton. He now had a free pass to cheat, and there wasn't much she felt she could do about it. She couldn't believe that he would even look at another woman. It just didn't make sense to her. She felt so vulnerable now that his feelings for her were in question in her mind. She needed to get this back on track fast but didn't know how. Everything she'd done before didn't work, so she needed a bigger plan. She was angry that the life she walked into in Jamaica had changed. She could only do so much more because she truly loved him with everything she had. She couldn't accept the new terms of their marriage, she was stuck.

Easton hadn't seen Sasha for more than a month. He was trying to make sure his wife was secure and settled into her new reality. He didn't miss Sasha at all, which proved to him that his trysts with her were in the right perspective. He could have her or not, and frankly would prefer his wife.

During his hiatus, he made sure she was getting an envelope and told that she would be called when he was available. He knew Sasha was needed and still had a purpose in his life. It had also been a month since he had been with Andrea, until she finally gave him the sign she was interested in having him back in her bed. She was extra loving with him now, giving him everything he'd missed while they were apart. She knew that, if she didn't give in, he had others he could and would see. So she gave Easton all she had to make sure he got the true loving, the love of a devoted wife, whenever he was home. He knew what was happening and enjoyed her competing with no one.

One night in the heat of their continued makeup sex, Andrea scratched Easton deeply with her acrylic nails across the side of his neck down to his chest. It was over the top and painful, but he didn't show disapproval; he allowed her to mark her territory. It was only fair, he thought, and kissed her through the burning pain.

Easton had been hanging around the house, and things were back the way they were before the day Andrea saw LaTrice. What she really wanted was to wind the clock back to when she was his everything, his

258

every minute. She was trying to pull him back into her grasp, and he was loving it. But Easton knew it was time to see Sasha. He thought about the four finger scratch down his neck but didn't care about Sasha's reaction. His wife wanted Sasha to see the markings, so he would let her.

He entered an upscale suite in downtown Kingston and greeted Sasha with a kiss on the cheek. He had ordered dinner ahead of time and scheduled it to arrive about the time he did. He knew he owed her the meal.

She was charming as usual and thanked him for the envelopes that made their way to her house. She was pissed off that whatever had happened with his wife had kept him from her a whole month. But he was there now, and she was on her job making him feel whatever the wife didn't.

Easton took off his shirt and did not try to hide the scratches. She noticed right away and knew exactly the message she was being sent. She was even more pissed now. She never asked him about it; she just got ready to do what he needed her to do. While wrapped in his arms, she softly kissed his neck over the healing cuts, acknowledging them to him in a way that said without words, it didn't matter where he'd been before because he was with her now. By giving affection to his wife's scratches, she was telling him she embraced the situation and her position.

It had been three months since Andrea had seen the photos, and all seemed forgotten. She and Easton took an afternoon off and played in the ocean outside their house like kids. She built him a sand castle and served him a picnic lunch on the beach, the same as they'd done in New Jersey. She had her radio blasting and a beach umbrella to shield them from the sun, trying to reenact her summer experiences at the Jersey Shore. *The only thing missing was crowds of people kicking sand on their food*, she thought with a smile. They enjoyed each other's company and living life their way.

The couple spent the evening dining on the patio, with Easton using his grill for the first time. They were alone, except for the dogs who were really enjoying the grilled meat Easton made. Andrea put a small box on the patio table and told Easton to open it. He reached across the table and took it.

"A gift for me?"

"Yup, open it," she said. He pulled the yellow ribbon from the box and lifted the lid. Inside was a pair of tiny yellow booties. Across the back of each tiny soft shoe was one beautifully embroidered word "Graham." He jumped from his chair so fast he spooked the dogs. He ran right to her side and laid on her. He was hugging her and the chair while squatting down in front of her.

Without lifting his head to look at her, he asked, "Is it true? Oh, my God, Drea! Please tell me it's true!"

"It's true, Easton. I'm pregnant!" It was the best day of his life.

Once the idea of having a baby sunk in, Easton couldn't think about or talk about anything else. All his thoughts were about his baby. He would see to it that nothing disturbed his wife, made her unhappy, or hurt her or his baby. This was the completeness he had longed for. He could feel it already, being a papa, a daddy, a father. It felt good.

· 30 ·

BLISS

The months were shooting by fast, and Andrea's body was growing. Easton couldn't have been prouder, and he strutted around like a peacock. She was now five months along, and they could feel the baby moving. She was worried at first about medical care because she was in the country as Tamara Williams with a fake passport, and the visitation date on her travel paperwork had expired long ago. Easton assured her that she would get care from an obstetrician that he would pay, and at the time of delivery, that doctor would admit her to the hospital and take good care of her and the baby. Andrea had her doctor visits on schedule, escorted by Easton with Sean not far away. She and the baby were healthy and on track for a normal delivery.

Soon they got the good news that the baby was a boy! She thought life couldn't get any better than it was at that time. But being able to give Easton a son took it over the top!

Easton made sure he was by her side as much as possible and provided her with whatever she desired. Andrea knew that now she had him back fully. He had not seen Sasha since he found out his wife was pregnant. He couldn't get enough of her rounding belly and his pride about being a father.

They furnished the nursery for their Jamaican prince with the finest imported baby items money could buy. Andrea was even more outrageous with her shopping than usual, buying herself chic and stylish maternity clothes in addition to top quality items for the baby. She wanted to look her very best for Easton. She was especially excited about a white crocheted maternity bikini with a matching crocheted sarong. She held it up to show Easton. "Isn't it just cute? I can't wait to wear it."

"It looks too small already," he said.

"I'm not worried about that. With this baby bulge, only you will see it anyway. Extra small clothing is sexy, right?" He shook his head at her logic.

Instead of Easton coming home late from his night meetings, he was now late going to the meetings, reluctant to leave her. His guards joked that he was back to being sprung now that Andrea was pregnant. One comment they spit out was, *"She know what she doin for sure, mon! Smart gal to get what she want. Him turn right and she make two lefts!"* They all rolled in laughter, knowing the comment wouldn't leave their circle.

· 31 ·

GWAN MAD

One very hot afternoon, Andrea and Easton were lying in the living room in the air-conditioning together on the large sectional couch watching TV. Easton lazily laid in one direction and she in the other. Andrea was falling asleep when the phone rang. Easton took the call in the kitchen and then moved with the cordless phone out through the newly paned French doors. Andrea wiggled up her now 7 months pregnant body just enough to see where he went. She hadn't gained a lot of weight during the pregnancy. From behind, it was hard to tell she was even pregnant; she was all belly. Miss. Merri told her she was very small, but with the next baby she wouldn't be so lucky; and with the third she would be the size of a house. After hearing that, Andrea told herself this would be the only baby she would ever have. One was enough to keep her husband tied to her. She watched as Easton made his way to the clubhouse. She knew it was business and didn't give it another thought.

Easton didn't utter a word on the phone until he reached his office out back. Seated at his desk, with his head lowered in his hands and the phone cupped between his shoulder and ear, he listened. The call was news that the Browns had a catastrophic situation that made a serious problem for King Louie and everyone who reported to him.

Things had been very tense in the Brown's camp since their monetary punishment had been handed down. The Browns handled the penalty at first, but when the restoration didn't come back after a year, a slow simmer turned to a boil. Number Two had the hair trigger, but Number One was in charge and could usually keep him under control. But now, with the state of their business, it didn't take much for him to pull his gun.

The caller told Easton that three European tourists had been killed in Kingston at the hand of Brown Number Two during a deal that went bad. Easton questioned how innocent people got killed during a private meeting. The explanation came forth that, Brown Number Two had shot a man in the chest at the negotiation table which started a massive gun battle in broad daylight that spilled into the streets of

Jamaica's capital. Easton tried to figure out why Number One allowed things to get so out of control. Now three innocent foreigners were dead. This would bring international media and governments in, probing the incident to the highest level imaginable. After the probe, they would likely call for the Jamaican government to serve up the offenders, which Jamaica would do for the sake of international peace.

He was relieved that the emergency meeting called that night by King Louie was scheduled for midnight, so he could go ahead with a surprise he planned for Andrea that night. He planned to be suited and ready for his drivers on time with no delays at 11:45pm, but after making his wife an even happier woman!

267

· 32 ·

WHO'S GONNA LOVE YOU?

Easton didn't want his wife going far from Hunter's Bay. He was paranoid that if she needed to see the doctor, she wouldn't be close to home so his surprise wouldn't be too far.

When he went back to the main house, Andrea was yelling to him that they should get Martha Jay's for dinner. She went on and on. "Can we get Martha Jay's conch salad tonight? That place makes the best conch dishes. I'm glad I found it and tried it. A lady named Martha from the Bahamas owns it. I met her the other day and she told me all about her country and good places to visit there. I really liked her, we should go to the Bahamas when the baby is born."

Quickly shifting back to what she wanted to eat, "Or maybe stuffed conch with the fritters and a frosty virgin Hummingbird to drink. *Mmmm.* That's what I want."

"No seafood Drea! Remember?

He went to the couch and told her that he had surprise plans for dinner and that she needed to get dressed.

"Where are we going?"

"Not far. Just put on a bathing suit with a cover up and maybe a bag with a towel and sunscreen. You know all that stuff you take down to the beach with you."

He helped her off the couch, and she eagerly went to get what she needed for the mystery date Easton had planned for her. She went through several dresser draws of bathing suits and came up with the white crocheted bikini she was so happy to get but hadn't worn yet. She squeezed into the bikini top and realized Easton was right. It was not going to fit. She shoved and adjusted her breast into it so that at least half of each was covered. The bikini bottoms went on with no problem because the waistband landed underneath the baby. She grabbed the matching sarong and wrapped it around her whole body, hiding the top and the bottom of the bathing suit.

Easton escorted her out of the French doors and headed to the beach. They stood at the water's edge holding hands, while Easton shaded the sun from his eyes with his other hand to look out on the water. "Well," she said. "What are we looking at?"

"Just keep looking."

Soon after, a beautiful white, sleek, 80-foot yacht came into sight. It was gliding on the water the way a stingray flies in the deep ocean. Andrea sucked in almost all the air around her as she gasped in awe at the beautiful vessel. Alongside it was a small speedboat that looked like a running child trying to keep up with a much bigger adult. Suddenly, the yacht stopped about a mile from the beach, and the speedboat continued heading towards them.

Easton turned to Andrea and said, "That boat is yours!" She couldn't believe the extravagance of Easton's surprise gift! If she could have jumped into his arms, she would have. But she settled for a quick hug and a kiss and took another look at her new yacht.

When the small speedboat made it to the shore, she realized why it was needed. They helped her wade through the shallow blue water, Easton on one side of her and one of the four guards that rode in the speedboat on the other side of her.

Once everyone was in the boat, it easily whipped around in a half circle and headed to her beauty sitting out on the ocean like a queen holding court. The speeding taxi boat left rushing white waves in its wake as it sped to the yacht. The tiny splashes of water bouncing from the front of the boat hit them, and it felt like a refreshing sun shower cooling the sting of the Caribbean sun on their skin. Once the speedboat sided up at the back lower deck of the yacht, Andrea was the first to take the built-in steps, as many hands helped her aboard. Easton was up next, and he easily jumped onto the landing. He turned her from facing the ocean to the back of the boat because she hadn't noticed the yacht's name. Painted in the prettiest swirling script letters stretched all the way across the back end of the boat was its name. It read:

Who's Gonna Love You?

Right underneath the name in plain letters was the boat's country of origin:

Jamaica, West Indies

Easton was proud of this finishing touch and couldn't wait for Andrea to see it. She was speechless and so grateful that she began to cry.

They made their way up another set of steps to the main deck. The anchored yacht hummed smoothly like an expensive luxury car. The boat was brand new, and the smells of leather, plastic, and a new engine permeated the air. Waving strong from the tallest pole at the very top of the boat was the Jamaican green, black and yellow flag. Beneath it was the United States flag. "*You see dem stars and stripes?*" he said while pulling her close and pointing up at the flags. "*That's yah flag. We will only fly it when you are aboard. What yu tink baby?*"

Andrea was still overwhelmed and in a complete state of shock and excitement. "I can't believe this, East," she managed to get out.

Toward the front of the boat was the captain Easton had hired to sail her boat whenever needed. The captain tipped his hat to them as they passed and said hello. Then, he returned to his duties. "The Who's Gonna Love You?" was magnificent and beyond Andrea's wildest imagination.

When the tour was finished, Andrea went inside to the sitting area that served as a living room. The air-conditioning was flowing, which made the cabin comfortable. Easton moved to the galley and started pulling dishes and food from the refrigerator.

"I thought we'd have an early dinner out on the deck and watch the sunset," he said.

"That sounds so romantic, East"

She heard the motor of the small speedboat start so she looked out of the window to see what was happening. The speedboat with all four of Easton's guards and the captain was speeding away toward the house.

"Where are they going, East?"

"Don't worry. They'll be back after dark to pick us up. I wanted privacy."

He brought her a wine glass with juice in it, while he had a beer.

"I can't wait to have this baby and be able to drink something stronger than juice and water."

"Not so soon baby, you need to breast-feed my son," he informed her.

"I won't be doing that. There are great formulas out there. I have to get my body back and not be attached to a baby for the first 6 to 9 months, East."

Her statements concerned him, but he decided to drop it for the time being and address it later, before his son was born.

Andrea looked out again and could see that the speedboat had made its way to shore. She saw the men getting out on all sides of the boat. She then brought her attention back to her loving husband to start their romantic dinner on her beautiful gift!

· 33 ·

FIREWORKS

They were all alone on the ocean now to enjoy her gift and to have a romantic afternoon and early evening. The queen was a lady and handled the waves with ease. She swayed slightly without moving anything around or making either of them unsteady. After their light meal, they laid on the deck in custom lounge chairs, lathered in sunscreen. Andrea took off her sarong, exposing her tiny white bikini so she could rub sunscreen under it.

"Oh, I like it," Easton moaned. *"Bring dat here."* He wrapped his arms around her and stooped to kiss his son in her stomach. The stereo was turned on and music was being piped through speakers on the deck. It was a perfect day and about to be a perfect Jamaican sunset.

While they watched the water, Easton told her about the late-night meeting he needed to attend.

275

"I gotta go about 12 tonight. This means I won't be back until later in the morning, since KL couldn't take this meeting until then."

"Oh," is all she said knowing she couldn't ask about any details.

"Yeah, it turned out ok, because I had already planned all of this. Later worked for me."

"Yes, that was lucky for us," she responded.

The sun slowly disappeared, and the yacht lit up like a Christmas tree. Andrea didn't think it could get any better, but it did. Now snuggled up on one lounge chair together, Easton pointed to the shore in front of their house.

"Look! See the men?" he said while pointing to the shore.

"Yeah, what are they doing?"

"They're setting up the fireworks to celebrate the coming of my son!" he boasted.

"Wow! Really, East?"

"Yeah, I did that, woman, for you and the baby!"

Just then, he had an idea and hopped up to shut down the inside and deck lights so they could watch the fireworks in total darkness from the middle of the ocean. Andrea could see people on the shore moving and setting up what looked like canons. They were the professionals lining up the rockets. The first one flew out like a missile and burst into beautiful white stars in the sky right above the yacht. The sound was loud but thrilling. One after the other, they burst in the sky, which was lit up in red, blue, white, and even purple just for them. Andrea thought, *This is it, the absolute pinnacle of my life. Giving him a baby was for him. But all of this, his arms around me, him loving me again, my yacht…this is for me!*

She had him back the way she wanted him, giving her and only her his love in and out of their bedroom. The spectacular show continued, and the power of the booms got louder, startling them. They weren't concerned at first because fireworks were usually loud, especially professional displays being operated by a team of pyrotechnics specialists.

The next explosion was a blistering sound that made them both duck, but when they looked up, there were no fireworks! Before they knew it, a large speedboat had run almost into the back of the yacht with a flurry of activity so fast they didn't have time to react. What seemed like fireworks that got a little too close to the boat was actually gunfire. As they tried to run for cover, the yacht was being riddle with bullets. Easton wasn't pulling her in the direction of the cabin fast enough, so he grabbed her up in his arms and ran as low to the deck as possible, trying to get her inside and to his gun. Men were boarding the yacht quickly, and he knew he was outnumbered. He would have jumped overboard and swam for the shore if it weren't for Andrea.

Once the guards on shore realized Easton and Andrea were under attack, they immediately jumped back in the speedboat and raced back to the yacht with guns drawn.

Easton and Andrea were held up in one of the bedrooms in a corner crouched on the floor. Easton was in front of her facing the door, holding his gun straight out, waiting for someone to enter, so he could blow their head off.

The shooting continued, and Easton muttered out loud, "Who are they shooting at? No one is out there!"

Just then, they could hear that Sean and the guards had made it on deck. An ear shattering gun battle was coming closer and closer to their bedroom where Easton crouched trying to protect his wife. They was trapped. There was nowhere to go. They were in the middle of the boat with no escape.

Andrea could hear Sean shouting instructions to the other men, but she couldn't make out what he was saying. Sweat was pouring off

Easton. He was waving his gun from side to side in the direction of the noise outside, even towards the wall in case they crashed through it.

Andrea was crying as quietly as she could, but the fear was too much. She knew Easton couldn't shoot them all if they burst through the door. Suddenly, the noise stopped. There was no gun fire and no shouting. The quiet was frightening, and the not knowing what was happening was equally as bad as the shooting. Easton turned to face her for the quickest second, not wanting to turn his eyes from the door.

"Shhhh… listen to me. It's gonna be ok. I need you to be calm, so I can take care you. If they come through the door, I want you to get as low as you can, as close to the floor as you can covering your head. It's gonna be ok. I love you, Drea."

He whipped back around and continued holding the closed door hostage with his gun. Suddenly, as he expected, the door knob turned. It didn't open because Easton had locked it behind him. One powerful kick, and the door flew open. Easton pulled his trigger several times, but no one came through the door. He knew at that moment he was a dead man.

He waited for the kicker to step in the doorway. It was quiet again. Andrea's entire body was trembling uncontrollably. She and Easton were smashed so tightly together in the corner she could barely breathe.

Then the gunman threw his arms and only half his body around the corner of the door and shot three times, hitting Easton in his torso. Easton's gun dropped from his hands as his body jerked backwards, thrusting him hard against Andrea who was now screaming.

The man who had just shot and killed her husband was a stranger to her, but she was not a stranger to him.

"*Well, now, all dis trouble was 'bout yu?*" he said.

She was looking into the face of Brown Number Two, Morris. Screaming and crying, Andrea started crawling toward the gunman as fast as she could, trying to make it past him and to the door. He caught her ankle and dragged her back towards him. As he snatched her up, he threw her against the wall. He was surprised she was pregnant. He looked her up and down in her tiny white bikini, staring at her belly. His eyes were wild and showed the disturbed mind that was behind them. Andrea was trying to get her thoughts together enough to make a plan but couldn't get her mind or eyes off of her dead husband now slumped in the corner bleeding, alone.

Morris whipped her around again, gripping her in a standing choke hold against his body. "*Walk and shut tup,*" he demanded.

She walked in the direction he was pushing her with his body. They walked out of the bedroom, leaving her Easton behind. They walked through the living room and onto the main deck.

Armed men from the Brown's camp were standing around admiring the three bodies of Easton's guards, dead on the deck. All the ship's lights were now on, illuminating the gruesome sight.

Brown Number One, Norris, looked at what his brother brought out from the bedroom with anger. "*Why yu brought her here? You shoot her back dear. No one left!*"

Morris tilted Andrea's head to the side and held his gun to her face and kissed her neck.

"I want her," he answered his brother.

"No!" Norris shouted. "Kill her now!"

Andrea trembled while they argued back and forth about her fate. She didn't know if she would be killed on the spot or raped and tortured first.

Just then, from around a corner, Sean flew out from his hiding place. He was shooting in every direction. First, he shot Morris in the head, splattering blood all over Andrea. Then, he hit Norris in the chest at point-blank range. Norris fell off the side of the boat into the ocean. Andrea dropped down low and ran to the other side of the deck and onto the catwalk where Sean had been hiding. The other men with the Browns were caught off guard and ran for cover. Sean quickly retreated back to the catwalk right behind Andrea, pushing her to move faster as they ran around to the front of the boat. Her crocheted white bikini was soaked with several different shades of blood that was drying. Sean gently guided Andrea to the front deck floor, making sure not to touch her belly. He was still respecting his boss' wife, knowing how Easton felt about her. Without a word, Sean squatted down, grabbed a life jacket from a deck bench, stuck it over Andrea's head, and quickly tied the strings. She was now trembling hard and moaning. He knew she was in shock, but there was nothing he could do. Three men were still alive on the boat, and he knew they would be coming for them in a matter of seconds.

He stood her up and then backed her up to the rail of the boat. Before he could take the final action of his plan, the men rounded the corner one by one, shooting to kill. Sean was able to shoot two of them before the other hid. Sean was hit in the side of his neck and was bleeding profusely. Before he lost consciousness, which he knew he would, he held his neck with his wrist with the gun in that hand. With the other hand Sean shoved Andrea over the rail. When the last man attempted to take a shot, Sean removed his wrist from his neck and pulled the trigger of his gun with both hands. The two last men of the battle were hit and fell dead.

Once Andrea's body hit the water, she was out cold. The gunfire ended, and the ocean was silent. There were dead bodies all over the boat and the smell of gunfire over took the air. For two hours, Andrea's body floated aimlessly, bobbing on the water. She was in total darkness floating further and further away from the boat. She had gone into labor before Morris grabbed her and she had been contracting and bleeding for hours. As she floated, her baby was dying. The JCF Police surrounded the yacht trying to figure out what happened. But it was too late to save anyone.

· 34 ·

THE FINAL CALL

A picturesque Cape Cod with a traditional white picket fence sat on a beautiful wooded hillside in Connecticut. Anyone driving by would admire the pretty flowers and perfect landscaping. The backyard was also impressive with lovely lawn furniture, a large garden, and a mass of mature trees framing the property. All that was missing was a few kids and a golden retriever running around.

Andrea stood at the kitchen sink washing a plate. She looked out the window above the sink into the backyard, thinking about new plants she could add or things she could change to make the yard even more perfect than it was.

Because she was bored with her suburban life, she was always looking for new things to do. She was now the three-glass-a-day merlot-drinking wife of Evan Livingston, Esquire.

When Andrea was rescued by the JCF Police six years prior, she was taken straight to the emergency room at the hospital, where she lost the baby boy Easton was so proud of. She told herself it didn't matter because she didn't want the baby without Easton.

Once she was stable, she was deported and told she was lucky she wasn't being charged as an accomplice to murder, drug trafficking, illegal weapons possession, and a host of other things they couldn't then charge Easton with. They kept calling her the American wife of the kingpin.

Two months after being back in the U.S., Andrea found Evan and told him the same story she told her father a few years before, that she had been in the Caribbean with friends to work at a hotel to learn about hotel management. She charmed him, got him to marry her, and settled right into the role of acceptable lawyer's wife in an upscale suburban town.

While she looked out the kitchen window, Evan came up behind her with a hug and startled her.

"Hey, what are you daydreaming about now, Andy?" he asked. Evan called her Andy like her father did, which she didn't care for, but she never complained. She snapped to and put on a fake smile as she always had.

"Nothing important. You set for dinner? It's almost ready."

"Sure thing," he replied.

"Did you hear from the agency today because they were supposed to call?" he asked.

"They called," she assured him.

"What's the latest then?"

"We've definitely moved to the final adoption stage. We're in the home stretch."

Evan and Andrea were adopting twin babies because Andrea couldn't conceive. Knowing Evan wanted children so desperately, she agreed to adopt twins who needed a home. She couldn't say no to her husband, but her heart just wasn't in it. They ate their dinner on time as usual and had their same basic dinner conversation.

"I'm full," Evan announced as he stood up and pushed his chair in. "I'm headed upstairs to take my shower. You wanna join me, sweetheart?"

There was silence. "Please," he added. She stood up too to take both plates to the sink before giving him an answer.

"Sure, I'll be up in a minute to join you. Just let me clean up the table, and I'll be right behind you."

With a hop in his step, Evan took off towards the stairs to get the shower going for him and his wife.

The phone rang before Andrea could finish cleaning up. She intended to let it go into voicemail, but on the third ring, she picked it up.

"Hello," her voice sang with a fake sweetness. Silence. Again she gave another hello a little louder.

"Drea!" said a deep voice that climbed out of the receiver and hit her in the heart. She fell to her knees right in the kitchen holding the phone with both hands tight to her ear as if the voice would slip away if she didn't squeeze. The only sounds she could make were several whimpers. He knew she was still there. He uttered only two more words to her.

"Soon come."

She only managed one word back.

"Now!"

About The Author

This is Kim M. Lindsay's first novel. Lindsay was raised in Central New Jersey and often includes areas where she's lived in New Jersey in her creative writing. After returning from college, she moved back to New Jersey and started writing. She also took an interest in photography. After publishing a photography book in 2009, she began to write her first novel. She now lives in Pennsylvania with her daughter.

www.ingramcontent.com/pod-product-compliance
Lightning Source LLC
Chambersburg PA
CBHW020412260626
47156CB00007B/2348